LAST WINTER, WE PARTED

LAST WINTER, WE PARTED

FUMINORI NAKAMURA

Translated from the Japanese by Allison Markin Powell

First published in English in 2014 by
Soho Press
853 Broadway
New York, NY 10003

Library of Congress Cataloging-in-Publication Data

Nakamura, Fuminori, 1977–
[Kyonen no fuyu kimi to wakare. English]
Last winter, we parted / Fuminori Nakamura ;
[translated by Allison Markin Powell].
ISBN 978-1-61695-455-0
eISBN 978-1-61695-456-7
1. Writers—Fiction. 2. Murder—Investigation--Fiction. I. Powell,
Allison Markin, translator. II. Title.
PL873.5.A339K9613 2014
895.63'6—dc23   2014014477

Interior design by Janine Agro, Soho Press, Inc.

Printed in the United States of America

10 9 8 7 6 5 4 3 2 1

Dedicated to M.M. and J.I.

1

"IT'S SAFE TO say you killed them . . . Isn't that right?"

The man's expression does not change when I say this to him. He is wearing a black sweat suit, his body leaning lazily in his chair. If the transparent acrylic glass weren't between us, would I be afraid? His cheeks are hollow, his eyes slightly sunken.

"I've had my doubts all along but . . . why did you . . . after the murder, Akiko's . . ."

—*Don't jump to conclusions*, he says.

He remains expressionless. He seems neither sad nor angry. He just seems tired. The man had been born tired.

—*I think I'll ask the questions, for a change.*

I can hear his voice quite clearly even through the acrylic glass.

—*Are you . . . prepared?*

"Huh?"

The air suddenly grows chilly.

—*I'm asking if you're prepared.*

The man is looking straight at me. He hasn't shifted his gaze once, not for some time now.

—*You want to know what's inside my mind. Isn't that right? . . .Why I committed a crime like that. You want to know about the deepest reaches of my heart. But up till now, nobody has come to see me in person . . . Do you know what that means?*

He moves only his mouth—otherwise not a single muscle in his face shifts.

—*That I would talk to you. And probably eagerly. Loneliness can turn a person into a great talker. You seem like you can manage to sit with me as long as you're on the other side of this acrylic glass. But here's what it feels like to me. Like we're sitting face to face in a small enclosed room, having a chat. Try to imagine it. Having a conversation with a person who committed a bizarre crime, and at such close range, listening to everything that's inside his mind . . . It would be as if I were putting myself inside of you.*

". . . Inside me?"

—*That's right. Whatever's inside me, it would end up inside you. Whatever's inside you would probably be activated by the process . . . As if I—a man who's going to be executed—as if I could go on living inside of you. Are you okay with that?*

"I don't know," I say honestly. "But I've decided to write a book about you."

The room grows chilly again. The place must be cleaned daily; although the floor is worn, there isn't a speck of dust on it.

—*Why? . . . Because you're also a member of K2?*

The guard in uniform behind him is staring at me. The walls of the room are starting to get to me. It's as though, little by little, the room is closing in around the man. I draw in my breath. I am conscious of the acrylic glass in front of me. It's all right, I murmur inside my head. This is surely an opening in the conversation. But the gap is small. We aren't even alone. And there is a time limit.

". . .I'm just interested in K2."

—*Interested . . . That could be dangerous.*

The guard in uniform stands up and informs us of the time. I let out my breath. The man is aware of my relief. He is watching me. He sees the state I am in.

—*Okay . . . You can come back again*, he says in parting. The door behind him opens.

—*But I'm still not sure whether I'm going to tell you anything. I'm not too good at analyzing myself. So.*

As the man is led away, he continues.

—*Together, I guess you and I can think about things . . . I mean, like why I did what I did.*

———

AS I LEAVE the prison, dusk is falling.

I take in a breath. But there is no freshness to be had in the exhaust-choked air. When I realize that I am fumbling around in my pocket, I still my hand. In the distance I can see the lights of a convenience store. The man's voice still echoes in my ears.

I cross a wide road that is wet from rain and go inside the convenience store. I stare at the cigarette display for a moment, grab a pack, and set it along with a lighter on the counter by the register. When I touch the gloss of the plastic-wrapped package, my fingers feel a trace of warmth.

The thin cashier takes the scanner and starts reading the barcodes with distracted movements. For some reason, I feel oppressed by the cashier's gestures. I go outside and light a cigarette. Even though I quit smoking.

My throat feels parched. This thirst is not likely to be quenched by water.

I scan my surroundings futilely and start walking. My notebook and recorder are in my bag. They feel terribly heavy all of a sudden. I hadn't been able to bring the recorder into the visiting room.

A hard rain begins to fall. The ground is already wet so this must have just been a temporary lull. People run to get out of the rain. They glance at me, standing there getting wet, as they pass by. Like they see something bizarre that they don't want to have anything to do with. I hold my hand over my head and start to trot. The fact is, it really doesn't matter to me whether I get wet.

Take another look at me, I want to say, but to whom I don't know. I'm running like this, to get out of the rain. Just like you all.

At the edge of my vision, I can see that the lights are on in a small bar. In the evening dusk, the lights seem tentative as they flicker off and then dimly back on again.

Just as a shelter from the rain, I try to tell myself. I draw closer to the lights of the bar. I open the glass door, which has no trace of fingerprints yet, sit down at the counter, and order a whiskey on the rocks. Bartenders are wary of customers who arrive just as the bar is opening.

"It's raining."

FUMINORI NAKAMURA

". . .What?"

"Uh, the rain."

I am at a loss for words. He serves me the whiskey, and I bring the glass to my lips. I put the liquid on my tongue, and the moment I feel the expanse of sweet warmth, I gulp it down. It is as if my throat has no patience, and needs to hasten it down all at once. The man on the other side of the bar is watching me. He must be used to seeing the moment when someone who abstains decides to give up.

"Are you . . . prepared?" The other man's voice floats through my mind. Prepared? I attempt a smile. I bring the whiskey to my lips again. As if I'm a ravenous insect. The warmth of the alcohol spreads to my brow and into my chest.

I don't need to be prepared. I have nothing left to protect.

Archive 1

Dear Sister,

Prison is not as bad as you'd think. But it's been quite a long time . . . I hope you'll forgive me for writing another letter like this. I can't help but get introspective in letters. I don't want to upset you all over again.

But I wonder why that is—why do people feel the need to reveal things? I don't know. Stuff about me has probably been wrongly reported out in the world. That doesn't matter. Because I don't even understand it myself—I mean, why I did such a thing. And why I'm going to be executed.

I hope you can forgive your brother. Well, to be more precise, I hope you can cope with it. But here, there's no chance of me coping with it all. I know I just wrote that prison isn't so bad, but there are exceptions. Like the nights. When I can't sleep, I get very frightened by this place. In solitary confinement in prison (those of us who commit incendiary crimes are thrown into solitary) the concrete walls and the iron doors that shut me off from the outside world seem only to heighten that feeling of terror. Every sound echoes coldly against the concrete and iron. It's the heaviness and the indifference of such hardness that scares me, more than being locked up in here. I wonder if you can understand.

Images of my own actions drift before my eyes. The heat of the moment, the sensation in the air—I experience everything as if I were reliving it. Down to the last trivial motions—even rubbing my eyes and swallowing my saliva. But in these visions, there are butterflies flying around me. I'm sure they're not real. But it's as though the butterflies are trying to disrupt the images I remember in my madness . . . It's almost as if they have come to save me.

———

Do you remember the first time I ever held a camera?

As far as everyone else is concerned, perhaps that was a fateful encounter—me and a camera. But a camera meant everything to me. Literally, everything. That's because I interacted with the world through the lens of a camera.

My first camera was like a toy, a black Polaroid. The first photographic subject in my life was you, my older sister. "Take a picture in case I disappear." You were only twelve years old, and that's what you said to me. I could sense the danger then too. If Father were to kill us, I wanted to leave evidence that we had been alive in this world, otherwise . . . No, that's a lie. That's not it. It didn't matter to me whether I lived or died. What I used to think was, "Even if he kills you, this way I can still see your face every day." You were always so concerned about what would happen if he killed you. What would happen to your little brother if you died. That's why you said, "I want you to take a picture of everything about me. Put all of me into this photo." Back then, sis, were you really just thinking of me when you said that? That wasn't all, was it? Of course it's true that you worried about me, but you—still a child yourself—you couldn't help but find it strange, the phenomenon of having your image appear on the page as a "photo," and maybe you were thinking that your self could be *transferred* into the picture? By doing so, you could find a safe place to go. Like inside the little locked closet in your room, or in the openings of the refrigerator or cupboard that no one paid any attention to, or outside, in the niches between the concrete blocks in our park, behind the flower beds . . . Maybe, if you could have, you would have left me and gone off somewhere.

Now I've grown up and won all kinds of awards for my photographs, but it's because of what happened back then. Because I was so serious about trying to get all of you into the photo when I was clicking the shutter. Over and over again, *I wanted to rob you of yourself* . . . Even if what was left was nothing more than an empty shell. I was trying to capture the entirety of you in a photograph.

It wasn't until much later that I realized what I really wanted was neither you nor a photo of you.

Sorry for bringing up bad memories. Thanks for getting me a lawyer. I'd just figured I'd have a court-appointed lawyer, so I am grateful. I don't like him much—even the watch he wears is hideous—but I guess he's better than nothing.

. . . Why is that? What's better than nothing? . . . No matter what I do, I'm going to be executed.

2

I FELL ASLEEP in my desk chair. Now I have a headache.

There is still some whiskey in a glass that has been watered down by melted ice. I had started drinking in that bar, and had kept on going even after I came home.

Thinking about how icy the water from the tap is in winter does not motivate me to wash my face. I start up my computer and light a cigarette. It is eleven in the morning. I wonder how long I have been asleep.

I look at the archived materials that have been converted

to digital format. Compared to how he looked when he was arrested, his appearance now is considerably drawn and haggard.

Yudai Kiharazaka. Thirty-five years old. Charged with the murders of two women, and sentenced to death at his first trial. The defendant is currently awaiting his appeal to the High Court. He had been a photographer by profession, but he only worked in fine art, and had mainly lived off of an inheritance from his maternal grandfather.

When he was young, he and his older sister had lived in a children's institution. Their mother had disappeared, and when the children had run away from their father, who was drunk all the time, they had been taken into protective custody by the police and then placed in the institution. It was unclear whether they were physically abused by their father, but both of them were suffering from malnutrition, so at the very least they had been neglected.

From then the records drop off for a while. It's unknown how the siblings were raised in the children's institution. But in due time the sister set out on her own and the brother started working at an auto parts manufacturer's plant while he went to photography school.

Apparently the Kiharazakas' mother had eloped when she married their father, and her family had disowned her. Even after she disappeared, there was no sign that she had tried to return to her parents' home. The children's grandmother had died, and their grandfather who was still alive refused to acknowledge his own daughter ever again; it goes without saying that he never recognized the children she had given birth to. But after his death, there were no other relatives to claim his estate, so the two siblings inherited it.

As a photographer, Kiharazaka is rather highly regarded. He has been selected for numerous awards, and four years ago he won a mid-level international competition called the Imre Award with a photo called *Butterflies*. At first glance, it appears to be a composite picture, but it isn't.

I open up the folder on my computer where I had saved the image. The photograph is a still from a film, and the whereabouts of the original photograph, along with the film, are unknown. The image I am looking at is a digital version that was published in a magazine when he won the award. When I click on the image, my breath catches. No matter how many times I see it, I still find it unsettling.

Countless black butterflies are flying about wildly inside a white room. Like smoke, the butterflies swirl in numerous eddies, seeming to burst from the center of the room and explode outward. Behind the disarray of the butterflies, there is a figure. A woman. But she is obscured by the shadows of such a vast number of butterflies. She is hidden. It is impossible even to tell if she has any clothes on. Or, at first glance, whether it even is a woman. But it definitely is a woman. I'm not sure why, but *I know that it is*.

"True desire is hidden," the Russian photographer who nominated the image for the award writes about the photograph. "Like Tarkovsky illustrated in his films, people's entire lives are motivated by their true nature, which they don't understand. When people look at this photograph, it inundates their inner selves. I don't know whether these butterflies represent divine goodwill, or the way that viewers willingly hinder themselves by their desire not to know their true character. When these butterflies disappear, in what way will the world that surrounds the viewers, who now know their true inner nature, be transformed?"

His critique continues as follows.

"The hidden figure appears to be a woman, but it very well may not be. It may not be a man, either; it may not have a gender, or very well may not even be a human being."

Certainly, it very well may not be a woman. But then, why had I immediately assumed that it was?

"There was a clergyman who prayed to God, asking for peace in the world."

The Russian critic goes on further.

"And God, knowing what the clergyman really wanted, granted with a smile not world peace, but something more like a naked little girl. If God, all powerful in his cruelty as well as his purity, had attempted to grant the clergyman's true wish . . ."

As I look at the photograph, my heart starts to race a bit. I put the computer to sleep.

Those who saw the original of this photograph on display in a gallery abroad had experienced something similar.

"This photograph looks just like an engraving."

"Like Van Gogh's oils, painted with thick brush strokes. Even though this photograph is two-dimensional, it has a physical presence."

I wish I could see the original. But its location is unknown.

I light another cigarette. Picking up the glass, I down the rest of the whiskey, which has been diluted by melted ice. I don't stand a chance against this without the help of one thing or another. The image of the photograph is still branded on the black screen of my now-off computer. I shut my eyes, but there it is again behind my eyelids. I move away from the screen.

Other than the desk, I have nothing but a simple bed. There isn't even a refrigerator in my apartment. It does not in any way appear to be the home of a living being.

How long ago did I lose interest in myself, I wonder.

As if to shake the thought from my head, I open my paper files. I decide to write a letter to Kiharazaka. If I keep meeting with him, I'll be consumed. First I need to know more about him. I figure if a send a letter, he'll probably reply quickly. Disturbingly fast. Like he has been waiting hungrily for it.

As far as interview subjects go, Kiharazaka alone won't suffice. His older sister is currently living on her own in Ueno. Will I be able to meet with her? It will be necessary.

And then there is Katani, the only person who could be considered Kiharazaka's friend, as well as the members of K2.

K2. Why had I myself been drawn to a group like that?

"True desire is hidden."

I try to smile but I can't.

Archive 2

Like I told you before, don't jump to conclusions. That's the only rule I want you to follow.

You're going to write a book about me. That's fine. But I'd like you to stop trying to intrude on my mind. Because . . . for the time being, I'm still human. I may be sentenced to die, but I'm still a human being.

Was that really your game plan? To get me to write it all in a letter? It's true, I do get chatty in letters. They make me introspective . . . It's not a bad idea. You must be a pretty sneaky guy. But I don't like the one-sided intrusion.

Why don't we try this. You share something about yourself with me. Don't tell me you've got nothing to say. You're the one who's so interested in me. What's more, you're a member of K2. In short, these are my conditions:

Instead of me sharing what's inside my mind with you, I want you to share with me what's inside yours.

You might call it *an exchange of insanity.*

How does that sound? I'm asking the question, but you really have no choice. You know that, don't you? At any rate, I'll start by saying a few things.

———

K2. What was that group about anyway? A bunch of guys who wanted their dolls; calling it a group provided the sense of acceptance they needed. But before I made my way to K2, I was a member of another group, a butterfly group. It was a small gathering of butterfly collectors.

There are butterfly collectors all over the world. Sometimes, people go mad over butterfly wings. And the butterflies, they dance through the air with those maddening wings. But the collectors—they chase after them, acquire them, and save them. One after another, after another. Unendingly.

There are many fascinating reasons for the various patterns of butterflies' wings—to attract the opposite sex, to mimic as camouflage, to threaten predators, or to imitate poisonous butterflies. The males are the colorful ones, so that they may attract the more modestly patterned females. I bet the butterflies never suspect that their own wings drive other creatures to madness—that is to say, humans who have no relationship with their sphere of life. By the way, the collective noun for butterflies is a rabble. Did you know that?

I've seen many magnificent specimens. For example, I saw the collection of an Irishman who was so crazy about butterflies native to Japan that he lived in the mountains of Nagano. His collection was brilliant. The rainbow of butterflies in his shadow boxes seemed to radiate their colors almost explosively. He was very proud to show off his collection when I asked if it was all right to take photographs. But then—I still remember this—before I was finished he made me stop taking photos. It seemed almost as though he felt like I was going to steal his butterflies. As if he were afraid that they would be absorbed into my photographs.

"They fill a void."

This is what the Irishman said after he stopped me from taking more photos.

"See, have a look. See the space in this shadow box? I can fit three more specimens here. I must fill this void."

That was a matter of course; however, once this shadow box was filled, he would just start up another shadow box. And fill it. His so-called void.

He was particularly fond of butterflies that have an eyespot pattern on their wings. There are many of these kinds of butterflies. Originally these spots were to threaten birds away, or another theory is that the spots purposely lure predators into attacking their wings—where they will do less damage—rather than harming their bodies. They inspire fear, and seduce . . . I thought the inner mind of that Irishman must have been quite a morass, for him to be so attracted to those types of butterflies.

I had no interest in mounting specimens. I was simply drawn in by the beauty of their wings, and I had figured if I hung out with these guys, who were collectors, I might come across some unusual butterflies. Photographs were what I was interested in. Photographs of butterflies.

Except there was a problem. It was a problem with the photos themselves.

I wonder if you can understand what I'm saying. Photographs capture a moment within continuous time. There was this butterfly, this one butterfly that drove me crazy. I caught this butterfly and kept it as long as it lived so that I could take photos of it. But there was no end to it. When I took my eyes away for a single moment, a single second, the butterfly would appear completely different to me.

I would look away from the butterfly. *For that instant, the butterfly was no longer mine.* Or when I photographed it from the right side, I couldn't capture its left side. That's why you think it would make sense to film it, right? Wrong. What I wanted was a single moment. I wanted a single moment of that butterfly. Yet for the butterfly, that moment was one of countless moments. And there was no way that I could capture all of them.

I spent entire days clicking the shutter at that butterfly. I must have fallen in love with it. I don't know. I put it in a cage and kept it, but I was in despair over the fact that I could never completely possess the butterfly. Well, actually, it was probably despair about the way that the world itself works. Why, when a "subject" is right in front of us, are we only capable of recognizing, of grasping, that one small part we see? That butterfly was the reason I was hospitalized the first time. I don't remember, but apparently I wouldn't stop taking photos—not even to eat—and when I collapsed, my sister was the one who took care of me. Then I went to the hospital. I was given a psychological diagnosis. Anxiety neurosis, I think it was. In the medical field, I guess they like to be able to put a name to it when people deviate from the norm.

I wonder if I've made myself clear about the fact that I have no interest in butterfly specimens. I don't understand why those guys like to collect and mount them. I mean, they kill the butterflies, thereby preventing any further possibility of their motion. Which means they will never possess the butterflies in their beautiful flight . . . Do you know what I mean?

K2. What I just described, that's probably the reason why I shifted my attention from butterflies that move to dolls that don't move. Then again, I can't necessarily be sure of that. But doesn't it make sense? I mean, who can say for sure that dolls never move, that they always appear the same way?

. . . I've rambled on. It seems as though your strategy worked out after all. I certainly do get introspective in letters. And on a night like this . . .

It's almost time for lights out. I can hear the sound of doors opening on the floor above me. Since I've been here, I've learned to figure out what's going on just by listening carefully. My hearing has grown more acute. It's as if my eardrums have become integrated with the hard concrete and steel doors. With a sense of hearing like this, if I were to get out of this place, I might not really need to worry too much about my sense of sight. Well . . . I wonder. Are they really the same?

Soon I'll hear the sound of footsteps coming this way. So I'll finish this letter.

Now it's your turn.

3

A ROOM AT a musty old ryokan. The elderly woman who showed me in spoke so softly I could barely hear her.

There are two cushions on the floor around a shoddy table. From the window, all I can see are the slender trees that stand right outside. A cluster of branches is too close to the window—the tips of the leaves are touching the glass. Although there are no actual tears in the paper of the shabby *fusuma* sliding door, a pattern that looks uncannily like a black forest is well worn into its surface.

Kiharazaka's older sister, Akari, was the one who—after I had contacted her who knows how many times—had designated this inn as our meeting place. She said that she doesn't want to attract attention. I don't blame her. She is the sister of a convicted murderer. Who knows what kind of connection she has with a place like this.

I open the window to smoke a cigarette. It seems as though the tree branches might reach all the way into the room. Taking my eyes off the branches, I am conscious of the recorder in my bag. I wonder if she will consent to letting me use it.

The *fusuma* door opens. A tall woman enters the room. It is Akari. I recognize her from an archive photograph that had been released by her family. Akari murmurs something, and the elderly woman who had shown me in nods and retreats into the corridor. Or perhaps there are two elderly women. It may be a different one than before.

Akari sits down across the table from me. My gaze is drawn instinctively to her eyes. It had been the same when I saw her in the photo. I feel the desire to look directly at something that I'm not supposed to.

". . . I am Kiharazaka's older sister . . . Akari."

"Yes, and I am . . ."

I hand her my card. She makes no effort to look at it.

"Um." Her voice is tenuous and low. "How did you find my address?"

She looks directly at me as she asks this. No idle chitchat or banter.

She is in hiding now. Her lawyer is functioning as intermediary, acting as shelter for her. I doubt anyone else knows her whereabouts.

But for the sake of this interview, I have the assistance of the editor at the publisher that plans to put out this book. They have their own means. Other than the police, that is.

". . . Because I'm working on this . . . I don't mean to be rude but I'm . . . Kiharazaka's . . ."

"You're writing a book about him. Why?"

She is looking my way guardedly. But why *am* I writing the book? She doesn't really look all that wary. It is almost as though she is pretending to maintain that expression, when inwardly she seems to be smiling. She is a strange woman. And I doubt I am the only one to think so.

"I'm . . . not sure myself."

"Is it because you saw that photograph? . . .The one my brother took, *Butterflies*?"

Suddenly I have an image of countless butterflies bursting into flight all around her. My heart is beating slightly erratically. I try to light a cigarette, but my lighter isn't working.

"Have you been captivated too? By that type of thing?"

". . . No."

"What is it you're looking for?"

She fixes her gaze on me again. There is something about her eyes. As if she is actually concerned about me. Concerned, and yet still trying to draw me in. She keeps looking at me as she opens her mouth to speak.

"Have you spent a long time looking at that photo?"

". . . No."

"There are people who say that it seems like it moves . . . Something, there in the background."

I have the urge to close the window. But it is too far away from where I am sitting. I feel as though the branches are coming in toward me. Countless branches, coming into the room.

". . . Is it all right if I record this?"

"No, it isn't. Please just listen."

My lighter is never going to work. I put my cigarette back into the pack.

". . . You and your brother Yudai have always managed to get by together. What kind of boy was he, when you were kids?"

She doesn't say anything. She just keeps staring at me.

"When you were kids, was Yudai . . ."

She maintains her silence. I have another urge to shut the window. This window isn't there to open onto the scenery outside. Instead it seems more as if it is there to protect the room from the trees that surround it.

Akari is wearing a red sweater over a black skirt. Beneath her dark shoulder-length hair, she wears tiny earrings that catch and reflect the light. Just when I think she is going to crack a sudden smile, she begins to speak unexpectedly.

"My brother used a camera as though it were merely an extension of his own body."

I can't seem to follow her pace. All there is for me to do is play along.

"Something that I thought was a little strange . . . when was this? . . . I don't remember, but one time . . . that's when it was. The two of us had decided to run away from our father—from home—and Yudai took my picture. And he said . . . 'Now it'll be all right.' That's what he said."

". . . 'All right'?"

"What could he have meant by that? Here's what I think it must have been. If we got caught, or even if we were killed, it would be all right because he had taken a photo of me when I was safe . . . That's what he meant."

I ponder what she says.

". . . I don't understand."

"I'm not surprised. At the time, we'd run away whenever we'd see a policeman. Isn't that strange? If we had just acted normal, he would have simply passed us by, but since we fled . . . that's how we got put into protective custody and placed in an institution. In hindsight, I guess that was a good thing."

". . . What kind of institution was it?"

"You know . . . the usual."

"Are there photos from that time?"

"None . . . I threw them all away."

She looks at me. Her eyes have a wondering look that is out of context with our conversation. Just what is it about this woman? I can't figure it out.

". . . You threw them away?"

"Yes."

"Why?"

She smiles.

"It must sound odd, but . . . when Yudai would take my picture, it made me feel strange. As if I myself were being cropped. As if my true nature were being stolen. It slipped away into the photograph, my real shape . . . I found this unsettling so I got rid of everything—all the photos my brother had taken of me, whatever I could find."

". . . Everything?"

"Well . . . there is a single photo left. But it's from when we were kids. It's the only one I couldn't bring myself to throw away. It's special to me."

". . . Since the first murder, you've maintained all along that Yudai was innocent."

"I still do. But . . . now that things have come to this, it's too late."

"About that photo . . ."

"You mean *Butterflies*?"

". . . Yes. Isn't that you, the model in the photo?"

She smiles again when I ask this.

"By modeling for it, Yudai was able, through you, to express his special feelings, I mean, feelings more than just between a brother and sister."

"You've got the wrong idea."

"Maybe Yudai was using you, to say something about your long-gone mother."

". . . Don't jump to conclusions."

I recall how Yudai Kiharazaka said the same words to me.

"And you're wrong. You don't know anything. At the very least you need to have the ability to understand that."

She continues to stare at me. With pitying eyes.

"You can't handle this."

"What?"

"You cannot simply come into *our realm*."

"*Your realm*?"

"There's no way you are capable of writing a book about us."

I again have the urge to shut the window. The branches are growing. Into the room.

"What a pity you are. Have you read Truman Capote's *In Cold Blood*?"

". . . I have."

"Really? I'm surprised. Capote wrote his nonfiction novel, and he lost his mind. Writing that book about the criminals who brutally murdered that family . . . At least he was able to finish it. I bet you'll give up halfway, won't you?"

The temperature in the room grows chilly.

". . . But you're still writing it."

". . . Yes."

What else could I have said? Consciously I draw in a breath. I look at her.

"That . . . the old photo, would it be possible to see it? The one of you and Yudai."

"It's in my apartment . . . Would you come over?"

She looks at me. With concern. And yet, she still seems to be trying to draw me in. A smile plays about her lips. She narrows her eyes.

"This is too much for you."

". . . I'll be there."

"Don't feel like you have to."

She smiles again.

"Another day, then . . ."

I LEAVE THE inn. For whatever reason, she stays behind in the room. Maybe there is something she needs to talk to those elderly women about. Why had she pulled such attitude with me, even though she is the one who is related to a brutal murderer? They are twisted, that brother and sister . . .

I rub my lighter over and over, until finally it produces a small flame. As I take a drag off my cigarette, the energy suddenly drains out of my body. I shake off a sense of eeriness.

The light on my cell phone is blinking.

I look at my incoming call list. Yukie.

She called fifteen minutes ago. What timing, I think.

Archive 3

Hey sis, the stuff about the trial, it doesn't matter anymore. Nothing's going to change my sentence. So I couldn't care less about anything in your letter.

Sis, how are you getting by these days? That's what I'd really like to hear about—what is your life like now?

Are you on your own right now, sis? After the first murder, you had said that you weren't seeing anybody in particular, but I sensed otherwise. You met a nice guy, didn't you. I guess it's kind of like brotherly intuition, but I'm often right about these things. I don't know what kind of guy he was, but he must have been a good person. I just have a feeling about this too . . . you've already broken up with him, haven't you, sis. And . . . yet again, my intuition tells me that very soon, you're going to meet someone else. Your letter just has the whiff of a man. I've got a feeling.

I'm sure you don't want to hear this from me now, but you have a bad habit, sis. You have a tendency to want to ruin people—or actually, you want to ruin yourself by causing ruin to others.

The other day I remembered something from back in school, when we used to make things out of clay in art class.

It was summer, and in the heat of the classroom, the clay model I had made had melted into the clay model that was next to it. Both of them were reduced to a puddle. There was nothing to do with them but throw them away. But as they were falling into the garbage can, I could have sworn that one of them—my clay model, that is—had been smiling. I didn't see the expression on the face of the other clay model.

Sis, you never fall alone. You're always caught up with someone else.

. . . Don't take it the wrong way. I don't depend on you, since I can no longer depend on anyone. I heard from the lawyer that you've suffered emotionally. It's my fault. I know that. It's all my fault.

I distinctly remember when you told me to throw away all of the photographs I'd taken of you. It was a shock to learn that my photos had always made you feel strange. But the truth is, I didn't get rid of all of them. That's why, now . . . I'm sending this back to you. I'm enclosing it with this letter.

Sis, you're my closest loved one. You're the only person in the world whose happiness I care about. It's all right. I'm no longer jealous of the men in your life. I just want you to be happy.

Isn't that right? Both you and I are hated by everyone out there. That doesn't mean it isn't frustrating, though. Being happy would be the best revenge . . . Be happy enough for me too.

I know about your bad reputation too. And about the nasty remarks you made to the victim's family after the first incident. But that was just because you cared too much about me. Right?

And already at that point, sis, you weren't in your right mind. You know . . . you've said all along that I was innocent, but you're wrong. I did it. I killed them. How many times have I told you? . . . I really hope you can forgive me.

You keep telling me to file an appeal. Just like the lawyer does. But there's no more use for me. Just be happy yourself. Let this photo be a clean break from me.

. . . It's a good one, isn't it? It seems like all of you is in here. This is one of the photos I'm most proud of. The young girl in a white dress, nervously facing the camera. Actually, you faced the whole world nervously, didn't you, sis? And behind this expression lies your true self. Everything is apparent on your face. I captured it all in that one moment . . . I think it's a terrifying image. It was cruel for me to have taken a photo like this.

Ultimately, sis, your way of dealing with the world is wrong. The same way mine is.

4

YUKIE DOESN'T JUST leave a message; there is also an email from her. A brief one.

> I'm not happy with you. Please contact me. Don't you think
> it's cowardly not to answer your phone?

Still, I don't reply. I need to break things off with her. I have known all along that a guy like me never should have gotten involved with her.

An old coffee shop. I am waiting for Katani. It is five minutes past the time we were supposed to meet. He is the only person whom Yudai Kiharazaka could call a friend.

I light my second cigarette. Weary-looking men sip their coffee without any apparent pleasure. I realize I am about to check the screen on my phone again, so I open the folder and delete her message. The moment I do so, as my finger touches the pads on my phone, I feel a slight sense of discomfort. Although it is only email, it is still completely erasing someone's words. Will my involvement with that person be erased as well? I sense someone's presence; I look up to see a man there. It is Katani. I stand up to greet him.

". . . I'm a little late. Uh . . ."

"No, it's fine. Thank you for coming."

Katani had been in graduate school researching mathematics, but he had quit suddenly, got his certification in accounting, and is now working for a mid-sized auto parts manufacturer. His hair is trimmed short, and he has a thin beard. He looks like one of the young people these days who are concerned about their appearance. He is tall.

Katani orders a caffè latte. I put my cigarette out.

"Um . . . Actually, I almost didn't come."

Katani shifts his gaze slightly downward.

"You're writing . . . a book about him? Will my name be in the book too?"

"I'll use an alias. You can also check the manuscript before it's published. If for any reason you object to something I've written, you can say so . . . Do you mind if I record this?"

Katani looks at the silver recorder on top of the table. It catches the light in the coffee shop with a cold gleam.

"Well . . . is it a problem if you don't?"

"No, not at all."

The waitress sets Katani's coffee on the table. It should have been a caffè latte, but Katani doesn't say anything.

". . . You've known Kiharazaka since you were elementary school students, right?"

". . . Yes."

"What was your impression of him back then?"

"Hmm."

Katani puts his hand in his pocket and abruptly withdraws a cigarette and lights it. He exhales the smoke. Calmly, quietly.

"Well, uh . . ." He speaks with a certain determination. "Why are you writing a book about him?"

He looks me directly in the eye until it seems he can't stand to anymore, and then he drops his gaze. The waitress passes by his side. Her white legs stick out under her short skirt.

"Because it's what I decided to do."

"But why? Are you fascinated by him? He . . ."

As he speaks, he meets my gaze again, then looks down again.

"He burned two women to death."

The coffee shop is poorly lit. I wonder why I chose this place.

"Akiko Yoshimoto and Yuriko Kobayashi. They were both so young. Why write a book about a man like that?"

". . . Because I have my doubts."

"About what?"

I light my own cigarette. I exhale the smoke. As if that is all I can manage. Katani goes on before I say anything.

". . . I had a bad feeling. He had transferred his obsession with his sister onto butterflies. That would have been fine. But then it shifted to dolls, before finally coming back to people. I thought it was risky. He put too much of himself into his photographic subjects. I recognize that's precisely what made him a brilliant artist. But it's a thin line, and dangerous if he were to cross it."

I am silent. Katani starts to speak again.

"Shall I guess what your doubts are?"

He is no longer looking at me. He keeps his gaze down.

"Why would Kiharazaka have murdered and burned his beloved photographic subjects? No, that's not quite right . . . It's horrific, but here is probably where your doubts really lie. When those subjects, I mean, when those women were on fire, *why didn't Kiharazaka photograph the scene?* . . . Isn't that it? Especially if that was *the reason why he burned them* in the first place."

I am positively speechless. I can feel sweat break out on my back.

"Are you familiar with the story by Ryūnosuke Akutagawa called 'Hell Screen'?"

I nod.

"It tells the tale of a crazed painter, who watches as his own daughter literally burns to death, and then he paints the scene. Afterward the painter commits suicide, but the folding screen that he leaves behind, with its depiction of hell, evokes a terrific artistry . . . Is this what you had in mind? If that were the case—if it were the mad act of a person crazed with his art—in a way it would be easier to understand. But that's not what he did. He simply burned them. Despite the fact that he was an artist, he didn't take a single photograph."

No longer able to stand it, I tear my gaze away from Katani for a moment and from a distance catch the eye of the waitress. Not having been listening to our conversation, she smiles. Unsuspectingly.

". . . I studied mathematics at university. I mentioned Akutagawa just now—I became interested in him and read some of his work because he had said that his writing required certain mathematical skills . . . Still, there is something familiar to me about that thin and dangerous line . . . Numbers are beautiful. They seem to line up coherently, but behind their logic lies an overwhelming chaos. And there is a pleasure to be found in proceeding to create beautiful order out of that chaos . . . Only, I knew the limits. I don't mean something as simple as the limits of my own mathematical ability. I mean the limits of my brain. Have you ever grasped the limits, not of your own skills, but of your brain's capabilities?"

". . . I don't think so."

"Most people are unaware of the true limits of their own brain. In reality, though, what would they do with that knowledge anyway? In certain areas of expertise, it's necessary to use the brain at the utmost limits of human potential . . . There's a fear of knowing just what that is. The brain tries to deny its own limits. Then numbers get distorted. Once, among the numbers, I discovered a formula that shouldn't have existed . . . It really was an odd formula. Not a breakthrough—because the equation was flawed, you see. But I realized that I was obsessed with the flaw itself. I was delirious with joy. That joy enabled me to keep working on the flawed equation, which brought me into strange territory. *I was thrilled when I realized it*. I was able to leave mathematics . . . To this day, I still wonder what the hell that damn formula was about."

Katani suddenly falls silent, as if he realizes he talked too much and is embarrassed. Or perhaps he is distracted by something serious. I think if I don't speak he won't say anything more.

". . . Kiharazaka's photograph, *Butterflies* . . ."

He doesn't respond to what I say. Despite the fact that a moment ago he had been speaking with such enthusiasm.

"For me, there's something about that photo of his . . . This all started when my editor asked if I might be interested in writing about him. That's how it happened, no dramatic connection. But then, just . . . when I looked at that photo, I realized I was on the verge of a morbid fixation on it. So the concept of writing a book on him is simply expanding the original assignment, taking it far beyond."

He still doesn't respond. It seems as though he might have regressed to the time when he was doing mathematics.

"I was interested in the man who took that photograph. Then I looked at the archives that were supplied to me. Both women were murdered. When the first incident happened, the fire was not treated as arson—but after the second murder, it became clear that he was responsible for both. It's not as if one could be deemed an accident and the other a murder . . . It's just like you said. I have various doubts, and that's one of them—why aren't there any photos of the corpses burning? Wouldn't an artist like him—one who sought out the bizarre—have been expected to take pictures?"

"I think you may have missed . . ." he says suddenly. "The relevant point here . . . You're subtly avoiding the question. What I wanted to know was, why are you writing this book? You said it was because there was something about that photograph. But that's just the semblance of an answer—there's nothing substantial about it. Pay attention to what I'm asking you now. *What was it* that drew you to that photograph? I would like you to explain by focusing on the question of *what it was* exactly. I expect the real answer is to be found there."

I get the feeling that he is not just an ordinary guy. It may not be outwardly apparent, but it seems as though something inside him might go off at any moment.

"You want to know what it was about the photo. I doubt the answer will satisfy you."

"All right."

". . . When I saw that photo, I felt like I wanted to push my way through."

As I speak, my heart pounds slightly.

"Through all those disruptive butterflies. I felt like I wanted leave everything behind, to push my way through those butterflies, and give it all up. It seemed to me that my own essence was to be found there. That until now, my

entire life had been completely distorted . . . I'm a member
of K2."

I take in a breath. As deeply as I can.

"However, I had never lost anyone close to me. So
there was no reason for the doll creator to construct a
memento doll for me. I had no interest in one of those
ridiculous real-woman dolls. Nor did I have any proclivity
for forcing myself on a doll . . . Nevertheless, I spent all
my time at his mansion."

". . . I don't understand."

"Right."

It has been quiet this whole time in the coffee shop. There
are several crude lights suspended from cords, and they
dangle like hanged men.

"K2," Katani murmurs. "I had been in regular contact with
him up until about when he was chasing after butterflies.
By the time he was in K2, when he had turned his interest
toward dolls, we had pretty much drifted apart. To begin
with, although we may have spoken to each other often, we
never had very meaningful conversations . . . You ought to ask
the other members about that period. You must know about the
time when he was hospitalized after taking too many pictures
of the butterflies. He was certainly acting strange after that,
but when he really started to go off the rails was probably
around the time he became a member of K2. He just . . .

Here's what he told me, a long time ago. '*Photography is an imitation,*' he said."

"... An imitation?"

"Yes, he meant, there is always an object. As opposed to something like an abstract painting, there is always a distinct object, beyond what you are seeing through the camera. Since you take a picture of that object, I guess you could say that the finished product is an imitation of that object . . . But he also said this: a photograph may be an imitation, but it transcends imitation."

Katani cracks a faint smile. I realize it is the first time I have seen him do so.

"Another thing he said is, art is a form of revelation."

"That sounds like something Sartre said. He wrote about how literature functions in the world—in particular how it serves to reveal man to the world."

Katani smiles once again as I speak.

"I don't know how he knows so much about so many things. That's just the kind of guy he is."

Archive 4

What you said about the inside of your mind was quite boring.

Because you're hiding behind your cowardice. It seems like you are refusing to share your true self with me—no, refusing to share it with yourself, even. How do you expect to intrude upon someone else's mind, when you yourself are cloaked in layer after layer of disguise? For most people, things are only ever permissible inside their own mind. The palatable dark places. Shady areas beyond censure. If people can accept those kinds of things, don't you think they'd want to read a book about whatever that might be for you?

————

. . . Last time I wrote, I made it to the point of the butterflies. Including the part about being hospitalized afterward. I'm not going to write about what you want to know until you show me your true nature. But I will give you just a little bit more. Why? . . . Because I'm lonely.

When I was in the hospital, there was a man there named R. He had lost his younger sister, and he had not been able to adjust mentally, so he had been admitted to the psychiatric hospital. He is the one who told me about K2. That there was a gifted doll creator. That he had constructed a sister-doll for him, but his family refused to let him be with it. It seemed that his family had put him in the hospital as a means of keeping him away from the doll.

He said that he could hear her voice. That he felt as though the doll were actually speaking to him. People who have lost a part of their body say that they can still feel pain in the limb that is gone, but he said that he could hear his sister's voice coming from the doll. And though it's extremely disgusting, eventually he confessed to me that he had become aroused by his sister . . . She said, Make love to me.

It must have been his own desire. By making a doll his lover, he could learn what his true desires were toward his sister. But he was a sensible person, so he could reject his sister's provocations. When he did so, the sister-doll then started saying that they should kill their parents. If their parents weren't around, it would just be the two of them . . . It's a good thing that he was hospitalized. But they almost put him in the single room next door to me.

My interest had been piqued, so when I was released from the hospital, I went to meet the doll creator. I'm sure you're aware, but I think most people are surprised at first when they meet him. They expect to see a creepy, jittery man, and instead here is this cheerful, unassuming person waiting for them. But that's just appearances. He's a genius. Those kinds of people are the most dangerous, as far as I'm concerned. When he showed me the dolls that he had constructed . . . I was amazed. It was the first time I had ever been so astonished by someone's talent.

I wonder if you've noticed? A particularly creepy tendency

about the way he makes the dolls? He doesn't attempt to accurately reconstruct the subject of the doll. He subtly emphasizes one trait that suits the client who has hired him, and then he goes on with the restoration. What the doll creator seeks is not integrity, but rather imperfection. The soul dwells in the distorted part, in the instability that maintains such imperfection. But it's a soul that suits the client.

Being a photographer, I was deeply interested in the work he was doing. In both aspects of it—that first there was an object, and that there was an art to creating an "imitation" in a particular sense. I took dozens of photographs of his creations . . . I was creating another imitation of things that were imitations themselves. At that point, I felt as though I had ventured into territory where what was original no longer mattered. Do you get it now? *The sensation of being in that place was very soothing.*

Why was it that you became a member of K2? Even coming up with a name for it was intentional. Don't you think? The doll creator must have wanted to lower people's resistance to purchasing a doll, even if only a little. To imply you're not the only one to buy a doll. You're not the only one who would do something like this. It means there's no need to worry, because there are lots of other members . . . But I wonder. There must have been some who, on the contrary, objected to being considered a member of this group.

In your next letter, I want you to be sure to tell me why you became a member of K2. Have you lost someone? Or did you love someone, someone whom you simply couldn't have? You must know about that stalker guy. How outrageous, asking the doll creator to reproduce a woman who still existed out in the world.

There was no way that he could have her. And yet, he didn't want to be a nuisance to her either. Of course, it's not like any of the dolls are made of wood. They're silicone. You can have sex with them, if you want. I wonder if he's still living with that doll . . . It's repulsive to imagine a life like that, right? But then, isn't everybody, to varying degrees, restored in some way? I mean, inside their own heads. A person who imagines having sex with a celebrity as they flip through a magazine's photo spread understands the actual existence of that celebrity, don't they? The mind makes up for what's missing. When a woman thinks about a man she loves, she is restoring him in her mind, right? To some extent, the woman tailors the image to suit her. It's simply one way of putting it—whether it's in our imagination or as a doll, we as individuals all have the potential to be restored in various ways. Don't you think?

I mean, in this world there are too many things we want that we can't have.

. . . Are you planning to interview the doll creator as well? I figure you'll go see him even if you end up giving up on this, so I have conditions. There are dos and don'ts about interviewing him. So before you meet with him you must make sure to let me know. Still, even now, I can't help wondering . . . How is it that a person like him is able to live his life, without ever violating any laws?

5

AKARI KIHARAZAKA'S APARTMENT. The scent of perfume is in the air.

In the dining room there is a table, with two long white sofas behind it. Between the sofas is a low table. There is no television.

". . . So you actually came."

She smiles as she says this.

"I didn't think you had the courage."

With her back to me, she pulls a bottle of wine out of the

rack. She is wearing a white blouse over a short black skirt. There is a design on her black stockings. It is a pattern of branches that look like they might strangle something.

She takes her glass and, rather than sit on a chair at the dining table, she sinks down onto the sofa. She hands a glass to me as well. When I take it from her, my fingers brush hers.

". . . This seems like expensive wine."

"Hmm . . . Does it?"

I begin to feel uncomfortable, so I take out a cigarette. But she murmurs, "No smoking."

". . . Sorry."

"No. There's no need to apologize."

She withdraws a cigarette from her own cigarette case and lights it. She smiles as she looks at me.

"It's okay for me to. But not for you."

There is a curtain drawn at the back of the room. I figure her bedroom must be on the other side. I take a sip of wine. The warmth of the alcohol spreads through my body.

". . . Kiharazaka's photo, from a long time ago."

"Yes, I have it."

She places an envelope on the low table. She takes out the contents. It is an old photo. A photo of two children.

". . . There's a resemblance."

"To what?"

"To each other."

A thin boy and girl are sitting on a bench in a park. The girl is looking somewhere off in the distance, and the boy is looking at the girl. Both of them wear vulnerable expressions. They seem as though they have been mistakenly left behind in the world. The girl has on a dress, and the boy wears a white T-shirt over blue shorts.

"Who took this photo?"

"Someone from the institution . . . I couldn't throw it away."

"It's a nice photo."

"Isn't it? But you can't put it in the book."

She takes a sip of wine. I realize that she must have been drunk before I got there.

". . . Do you want a cigarette?"

". . . No."

"I see. Well, you can't smoke."

She smiles.

"Actually, there is another photo . . . Yudai sent it to me a while ago. I think he had kept it to himself, this photo of me . . . I was very surprised."

"Where is that photo?"

"No," she says. "I won't show it to you. I hate that photo. It reveals my true nature . . . Ruthlessly."

"Your true nature? . . . What do you mean?"

"Well . . ."

She stares at me. With concern. But as if she is trying to draw me in. Softly, she begins to speak.

"You've been giving me that look all along."

I catch my breath. My heart starts to race.

". . . What look?"

"Longing. Like you want me . . . You ask a lot of questions for a coward."

She settles more deeply into the sofa. Distancing herself a bit from me. Her legs are uncrossed. Gently she smoothes the hem of her skirt.

"Ever since you first saw me . . . Possibly ever since you first saw my photo. What kinds of things have you been thinking about? Having your way with me, in your own mind?"

". . . Have I bothered you?"

"Another question."

She reaches toward the envelope that is on the table. I grasp her hand. Her cold, slender fingers. She parts her lips.

"But you have someone special . . . Yukie."

Instinctively I look at her.

"How do you know that?"

She smiles as she pulls her hand away.

"I investigated. Didn't you, too? Wouldn't it be unfair if I were the only one being scrutinized? You shouldn't be looking at me that way when you have such a special person in your life."

She keeps looking at me. With concern. Under her blouse, an orange bra shows through.

". . . It's over with her."

"You're a bad liar. Bad liars bore me."

She stands up.

"But anyway, you can't handle this. I would require a much bigger commitment from you."

". . . What do you mean?"

"Well . . . It would be bold of you even just to imagine it. Isn't that right?"

She looks at me with concern again. Then she turns her back on me and walks toward the curtain at the back.

". . . Please leave now. I'm going into the bedroom to change."

She turns around.

". . . Or would you force your way into my bedroom?"

She smiles as she says this. I am badly shaken, and she is watching me with pity.

". . . Would you grab me while I was changing, strip me, hold me down while I resisted, and make love to me? . . . Would you kiss me against my will, not caring as I struggled against you, putting your hands all over my body, using such force until I ultimately submit to you . . . That would be way too much for someone with such a naïve little girlfriend."

She goes into the bedroom. I stand up and follow her,

putting my arms around her from behind. I kiss her. As hard as I can. Her arms wrap around my back. Her tongue moves around gently inside my mouth.

". . . I thought you didn't want me to."

She pulls her lips away to speak.

"If you do all those things to me, I won't let you go. Not until you are completely ruined."

She looks at me as if she pities me for being as worked up as I am. With that same look on her face, she brings her lips close to mine again. Her tongue intertwines with mine. She keeps her eyes narrowly open and, while continuing to stare at me, she kisses me as if she were inhaling me. I caress her breasts. Her scent wafts through the room. I let my lips trail across her neck. She unfastens the belt on my pants.

"You'll hate me soon enough. You're still not ready for this."

As she speaks, she touches my penis. Caringly, as if she is even more concerned about my penis. Watching with studied amazement, now that I am so erect. She moves her fingers up and down.

"If you leave that girl Yukie, I'll do it for you. I'll do anything for you. But . . . not today."

She keeps moving her fingers. Warmth and pleasure rise up. Her tongue darts into my mouth again.

"Do you like it like this? Or this way?"

Her lovely slender fingers entwine around my penis,

tightening as they move up and down. It becomes impossible for me to keep a thought in my head. The pleasure builds up in my penis. I bury my face in her breasts.

"If we keep at this . . ."

"Go ahead and come. . . . Come! Come like a fool."

She murmurs in my ear. She places a towel over me, while she continues to move her hand. The movement of her fingers becomes intense. My breathing is ragged, I can't take it any longer. I try to stop her hand, but she won't let me. We kiss again and again. The pleasure intensifies, and I close my eyes. I ejaculate into her long slender fingers and the towel. My body quivers faintly with lingering pleasure. She strokes my face, and kisses my ear.

". . . Feel better? Now go home."

She is still smiling as she pulls away from me and stands up. She looks down at me.

"Come back again . . . And," her breath catches a little, "save me."

6

THE LIGHTS IN the room are glaring on the transparent acrylic glass.

Yudai Kiharazaka looks tired again today. He wears a black sweat suit, the same as last time. He is looking straight at me with his lifeless eyes.

— . . .*I had a lot of things I wanted to say if I ever saw you again.*

Again, he manages not to change any part of his expression besides his mouth.

—But there's something more important. . . . Have you met with my sister?

Behind him, there is a guard in uniform this time as well. He is not the same man as before.

"Yes . . . Because I'm writing the book about you."

—Is that all?

Suddenly I can feel the movement of her fingers. Her long slender fingers. I can also feel her breath. And the warmth of her body.

". . . That's all."

—That's a lie . . . Are you . . . prepared?

I maintain contact with his lifeless eyes. I can feel the pressure—I want to look away but I hold out.

". . . What do you mean?"

—You don't know about my sister . . .She's not the kind of woman you can just simply flirt with. Two men are dead because of her. So far.

My heart starts to race. I have the feeling that he is looking directly at my chest. As if he is trying to ascertain how fast my heart is beating. Her fingers grip around me again.

". . . Dead?"

—Suicides. My sister drove them to it. I don't know the details though. There must be more of them who attempted suicide, who didn't die . . . Quite the siblings we are, huh? You're in danger too.

The smell of disinfectant wafts up from the cold floor. As though no matter how persistently someone has tried to kill whatever germs are there, they still refuse to be eliminated.

—*I try to capture a person's true nature in a photograph. My sister . . . she stimulates a person's true nature, and throws it into disarray. In a way, I'm probably no different. My sister wants everything from a person. And when she's gone, the man is ruined . . . These men give up everything for my sister, and she sucks them dry, and tosses them aside . . . She's a looker, isn't she? My sister.*

". . . She's alluring."

—*Right. You probably think that you've never met anyone like her in your life . . . I want my sister to be happy. But it will never happen. I doubt she will ever be happy, or that anyone around her will ever be happy either.*

I am aware of the prohibited recorder I am carrying.

"She showed me . . . a photograph. A photo of you and Akari when you were kids."

— *. . . I was in it?*

"Yes. You were."

—*I have no interest. If I'm in the photo, then I didn't take it, right? So it means nothing to me.*

He lets out his breath. Still he doesn't shift his expression.

— *. . . But it's strange. That my sister likes you, I mean. You* *don't seem like her type . . . I wonder what has changed in her life.*

Suddenly, my reflection in the acrylic glass overlaps with his face. I look away. "Save me." I haven't been able to get what she said out of my mind. Her scent is still on my neck.

"Is Akari . . . is she in some kind of trouble?"

—*Hm? . . . It wouldn't surprise me if she were. She's the sister of a murderer. I've only made things worse for her.*

I wonder if that is all. I have the feeling it is something else. It doesn't seem like it is just some kind of abstract wish for me to save her from herself.

"But other than that, something more tangible."

— *. . . Did she say something to you about it?*

"No, I just . . ."

The man is staring at me.

— *. . . She made some bitter remarks to the bereaved families and . . . she has a lot of enemies. That's why she's living like she is, in hiding. Even though she had nothing to do with what I did, well, for instance, there are still the families of the men who committed suicide . . . Taking sides with my sister means everyone else becomes your enemy . . . But that's not what I meant by being prepared. Will you promise me something?*

There is a flicker of strength in his eyes. It is only the slightest shift, however, there is definitely emotion behind it.

—*Whatever happens, I want you to stay by my sister's side.*

Whatever happens. Even if she goes into a hysterical rage, even if she has an episode.

". . . An episode?"

—*Yeah, you really don't know what you're dealing with yet . . . If you're not willing to take on everything that comes along with her, then I don't want to see you again. Take it or leave it. But you ought to see the photograph I took of her. See her brutal past . . . I don't know if you could take it. Me, or my sister.*

His expression quickly returns. Back to apathy.

—*. . . When you're involved with my sister and me, you . . . Will you be swallowed up, and lose yourself?*

7

I AM READING through the archives, but my brain isn't processing them.

Of course it must be because I am drinking. I leave the archives on the desk and lie down on the bed. I can hear my neighbor coughing on the other side of the wall. It sounds like a painful cough, one that will dislodge something from deep within. He coughs again and again; it goes on without end. Wanting to get away from the noise of his coughing, I roll over. Keenly aware of the stranger who is just on the other side of the wall, I suddenly get the creeps.

My cell phone rings, and looking at the screen, I see that it is Yukie. I wonder why I didn't turn off the ringer. The high-pitched hard sound echoes within my small apartment.

Yukie will never be happy with me. She should just get rid of me and find someone new, I think selfishly. I no longer even know whether I love her. I want her to be happy, but no sooner do I have the thought than the intensity of my feelings is likely to disappear.

But the world around me keeps moving, regardless of my will. The phone doesn't stop ringing. As if it's reproaching me for running away.

I turn on my computer and look at Internet news I care nothing about. I read the biased comments written below the articles, and look away when they make me sick. The phone keeps ringing. The sound reverberates through my cramped apartment. I take a sip of whiskey and light a cigarette. I can no longer hear the coughing from the apartment next door. It is almost as though the guy is holding his breath while he listens to my phone ringing. As if he has stopped his coughing and is patiently, resentfully waiting. "Save me." I remember Akari Kiharazaka's voice. While the phone rings, I feel her fingers on me, hear her voice. As if she is right in front of me. The phone stops ringing.

In the now quiet apartment, my heart has started to race slightly. Through the wall I can hear the coughing start back up again. I get up, consciously draw in my breath, and grab my exhausted-looking cell phone. When I touch it, the over-worked device still retains the slightest heat. I call the publisher. I want to investigate Akari Kiharazaka further. I need more time. I have the guy with a deep voice who answers the phone call the editor who is in charge. He isn't there. That's how it always is with them, I think. Despite the ridiculous number of times the editor called to hound me to take on the project, whenever I try to reach him, I can never get him on the line. He doesn't even have a cell phone. I have no choice but to send him an email; he always takes forever to reply.

I am thinking about visiting the children's institution where Akari Kiharazaka had lived. I wonder if anyone who was there at the time will still be around. Her scent spreads across my chest. I wonder why she seduced me.

Just then the doorbell rings.

The sound seems too loud for my quiet apartment. My heart starts to race a little again. Could it be Yukie? I wonder as I approach the door. But it could be Akari Kiharazaka, I think. What will I do if it is her? Most likely I will lose any hesitation the moment I see her. I'll let her into the apartment and probably throw her onto the bed. If she tries to tease me or laugh, I'll show her my dark side.

Amid the contemptuous roar of the rest of the world, together she and I . . .

I look out through the peephole. As if I am a criminal peering out at the money I am about to steal. There is a man I don't know standing there.

Before I know it, I am opening the door. After I have done so, I realize I haven't latched the chain. Just what do I intend to do if this guy turns out to be dangerous? But the man just stares at me, without trying to come inside. He is wearing a grey coat over a navy blue suit.

". . . Who are you?"

"We spoke on the phone . . . I'm Saito."

He is a member of K2. I have been trying to interview him for quite a while.

". . . Why are you here?"

"I don't know."

The man is standing there, immobile. What is this guy doing here? He looks at me with jittery eyes.

". . . Just a minute, please. I'll get my things. We can go to a coffee shop in the neighborhood."

"Here is fine."

He keeps staring at me.

". . . Here? My apartment?"

"Yes. I don't mean to intrude on your privacy, but don't you want to be somewhere safe?"

This is a strange visit. I start to feel nervous. But why should I? I smile.

"No, come in. There's nothing here though."

The man enters my apartment. He looks around the room. There is almost no furniture. I offer him the chair from the desk, but he stands there without moving.

"Aren't you a member of K2? There's no doll here."

". . . I don't know if I'd call myself a member, I just hung out a lot at the doll creator's house."

". . . That's not the way I understood it."

He stands there with his coat on. Both his suit and his coat are new, and tasteful. His features are relatively refined. If I saw him on the train, I would probably take him for a respectable company man.

"Just thinking about giving you an interview is enough to make me depressed. That's why I figured, just hurry up and get this unpleasantness over with. Quickly. Before I change my mind."

"I appreciate your allowing me to interview you."

"The thing is . . . I'm also to blame."

"To blame?"

"No . . . That's enough about that."

I am just about to make some coffee for him when suddenly he moves.

". . . I just can't. It's got nothing to do with me."

"What?"

"Excuse me. I can't do the interview."

He makes as if to leave. I don't understand what is going on. My cell phone rings—it is probably my editor calling. But I don't have time to answer it now.

". . . Please wait. At least let me walk you to the station."

I run after the man as he leaves my apartment. I don't even stop to lock the door. I soon manage to catch up with him.

He wants to talk, I think. People like him sometimes turn out to be chatterboxes. As if they overflow when their isolation is suddenly broken. Drawing abreast of him, I make a suggestion.

"Why don't we go someplace else? . . . We can have a drink somewhere. It'll be on me."

8

WE ARE SEATED at a table at the back of a dim bar. I asked
for a beer, but Saito has ordered a whiskey. An oversized ceiling
fan is spinning above us without a sound.

"So you're writing a book about Yudai Kiharazaka."

He speaks softly, almost muttering.

". . . You mean, you want to know about the psychology
behind the crime. Like all those other nonfiction books . . .
where you interview all kinds of people in order to expose his
dark secrets . . . That kind of thing?"

He is right in front of me, asking these questions, but for some reason he seems to be looking at something behind me.

". . . Yes."

"Would my name be in it? Would I be able to check the manuscript?"

"You would, and I wouldn't put your name in it. Whatever I would write about you, there'd be no way for anyone to know it was you."

A woman in a short skirt brings over the beer and whiskey. A black bra is visible through her white blouse.

When the woman approaches our table, the man suddenly looks down. It's as if he's just trying to make it through the moment. First she places my beer on the table and then she sets down the glass of whiskey. While she does so, he doesn't move. He seems to be waiting to confirm that she has left, disappeared again behind the counter. After a moment he brings the glass to his lips and takes in a quick breath.

". . . First let's get something straight . . . I didn't kill her."

". . . Yes, I know that."

He is that woman's stalker.

"It was a traffic accident. I had absolutely nothing to do with it. It happened while she was on a trip with her bartender boyfriend. I don't know. By that time, I no longer had any interest in her herself."

". . . Because you had the doll?"

"That's right."

He drinks his whiskey. I am the one sitting across from him, I am the one interacting with him, yet he won't look me in the eye—it is as if he is having a conversation with someone else.

". . . She wouldn't have anything to do with me. But I was sure that was only because she didn't really know me."

He brings the glass to his lips again. The tone of his voice quickens a little.

"I thought that, in order for her to like me, I needed to know more about her. I was shocked when I heard the police use the word stalker."

Saito shifts his gaze somewhat to the left of me.

"I didn't think I was a stalker. I mean, stalkers are guys who are hated and feared by women. But I'm not like that. She just didn't know me, that's all, and she would like me once she had a chance . . . But, isn't that what a stalker says? I was devastated."

I nod vaguely. If I am overly sympathetic, I will come off as unnatural. The slowly turning ceiling fan casts a shadow over the right side of Saito's body at regular intervals.

"But, you know, I really loved her . . . I doubt you could understand. I didn't think it was worth living in a world where she didn't exist . . . But you know, I never wanted to cause any trouble for her. I just really loved her smiling face."

"I saw a photograph of her. She was a beautiful woman."

"You don't understand. Nobody else could fathom her true charm," he says absentmindedly. "It pained me to cause her grief. But, I needed her. I wanted her so badly and there was nothing I could do about it. When I saw her walking with another man . . . Anyway, you know what I mean, don't you? I attempted suicide. But I didn't die. Because I was a coward. After that, things got worse and worse for me. Her smiling face that I had loved, it meant nothing to me anymore. I even thought about killing her along with myself. I couldn't bear the idea of her being with another man. If I were to kill her, I'd have to kill myself too—I'd have no choice but to die."

". . . Is that when you met the doll maker?"

"I never thought he'd be such an unassuming person . . . To be honest, I had just figured I'd listen to what he had to say. I couldn't imagine the prospect of living with a doll. But then when I saw his collection, I was stunned. I couldn't believe how beautiful they were."

Saito's eyes are moist from the alcohol.

"Strangely enough, they were actually more appealing than real women . . . I gave it a shot and asked him if he'd make one for me. A doll that resembled her . . . But at that time, the doll maker said that was taboo."

". . . Taboo?"

"That's right. He said that he had never created one based

on a living person before. That it was very dangerous to do
so. And that he was committed to creating the dolls so that
people would never forget those who had passed away . . .
Yet he made one for me. He must have realized the dreadful
state I was in. That's just how kind a man he is."

Saito smiles vaguely.

"When I saw the finished doll . . . I was really surprised. It
was her, right there in front of me. In fact, the doll was even
more beautiful than she was in real life. The doll was smiling.
I don't know if it was directed at me but she was smiling all
the same. As if she accepted all of my madness . . . But I
know about the rumors. That I was hearing voices."

He stops suddenly at that point.

". . . What do you mean?"

"To kill the real her."

Saito is staring absentmindedly at something just off to
my left.

"I knew I couldn't do it. Still, she kept telling me to . . .
You think I'm a lunatic, don't you? But . . . that really doesn't
matter. Who cares what everybody else thinks is normal? . . .
But I wouldn't cross that line. Because, like I said before,
I was a coward. Then, the real her died. As you know, it
was bad luck. All because that stupid bartender was driving
drunk, even though she was in the car. But—can I tell you
this? This is a horrible thing to say . . ."

Saito looks directly at me for the first time since we have been in the bar.

"I wasn't the least bit sad. And that's not all . . . *From then on, the doll began to look even more beautiful.*"

He is still looking at me.

"*And to make matters worse, I told this to Yudai Kiharazaka.*"

"Kiharazaka? You knew him?"

"Yes. I saw him a few times at the doll maker's mansion. That's when . . . I told him about it."

Saito looks down.

"That's what I meant when I said that I was to blame. Because I talked to him about this. That's the reason I agreed to your interview. I couldn't let it go as if it were someone else's problem."

". . . What do you mean?"

"What?" He looks at me again. "What are you saying? Haven't you interviewed him yourself?"

"I have, but . . ."

"I'm surprised. This is too much for you. Writing a book about him." Saito raises his voice just a little. "Do you happen to know the kind of effect people have on him?"

"What?"

"You have no idea. He . . . *He has no desires.*"

I am distractedly watching the shadows that continue to appear on the right side of his body.

"But Yudai Kiharazaka, he's so obsessed with his photography that he would do that, kill two women."

"Yes, he certainly is intense. But his intensity is different from his desires. Nothing exists there, inside his mind. You're mistaken about him."

Saito stares at me.

"This is too much for you. You should go and talk to the doll maker. He can probably speak to you logically about Kiharazaka. I bet you'll learn something besides the facts you want to know. Also, Kiharazaka may be intense, but *how did his madness turn him into an actual murderer?* . . . That's something I just can't understand. No matter how easily influenced he may be."

"How did his madness turn him into an actual murderer . . . ?"

"Right. He didn't take any photographs of their deaths, he simply gave in to the violence and was consumed by it. *What could have possibly happened to him?*"

Saito suddenly stands up.

"In any case, that's all I have to say. I don't want to talk about this anymore. But . . . I'm also to blame."

"Please wait."

I also stand up. He looks at me. As if for some reason he feels sorry for me.

"If you'll forgive me, I'll ask a different question. This may sound strange . . . But you . . . you seem like a guy who would be popular with women. Please, I hope you're not offended, but you don't look like the kind of person who lives with a doll."

He stands there for a moment, and then he sits down again resignedly.

"Your question is uninteresting."

". . . I apologize."

He smiles vaguely again at my words, and then replies.

"For example . . . Even if you loved someone to death, even if you thought there was absolutely no one else besides that person . . . after you break up with that person, eventually you would be able to feel something like that for someone else. Because otherwise, it would be impossible to go on living . . . Isn't that right?"

". . . Yes."

"Love is not absolute. But such incomprehensible things are rare in this world. I've had normal relationships. I meet someone, then we break up, and I wallow in it . . . But she was really special. I never thought I would turn into a stalker. Well, I guess I've always had the potential for that sort of inclination, but . . . Anyway."

Saito stands up again as if indicating that he intends to leave this time, no matter what I say.

"The real her is no longer here. I . . . I prefer 'dolls' to people. You seem like a pretty happy guy, so I'll tell you just one thing. When I used to be with women, sometimes I would have trouble, you know, like ED . . . But now, with the 'doll,' that hasn't happened once."

That vague smile.

". . . But you shouldn't put that in your book. People wouldn't like that. Don't you agree? You have to write in a way that will satisfy many people, by distorting human darkness and light—the way they do in manga. You ought to be well suited to that."

9

I EMERGE FROM the narrow alley and cross the railroad crossing.

I am drunk, with no idea why.

Maybe I am feeling depressed. Maybe I am exhausted from all this investigating Kiharazaka. A happy guy? What was that guy Saito talking about? Aren't I just trying to take a look at other people from my own dark place? These thoughts float and hover, echoing stubbornly in my mind.

The tattered remains of a campaign poster pasted on a wall

is swaying in the wind. I turn left at the corner, cut through a parking lot, and come to stand beside a telephone pole. Directly in front of me I can see Akari Kiharazaka's apartment building.

I take out my cell phone and dial her number. My throat feels dry. With the cell phone pressed to my ear, I look up at her building. The thought crosses my mind that I want her to take me and devour me. Whatever I am hoping for, I don't care if she just uses me however she sees fit.

"What's the matter?"

I hear her thin voice through the receiver. She sounds formal and distant.

". . . I wanted to see you. Can you meet me?"

". . . I can't."

I am still looking up at her building, at the second apartment from the left. A dim light is on.

"Why not? I want to see you."

". . . You just want someone's permission."

She laughs. As if letting out a breath.

"You want me to erase your sense of guilt for cheating on your girlfriend? . . . I have no interest in sleeping with a guy who calls me just to see which way I might go."

The sky is overcast with dreary clouds, even the moon is obscured.

". . . I'm right outside your building now."

".... Hmm."

"I'm coming up."

"You can't tonight . . . Another man will be here," she says softly.

". . . That's a lie, isn't it?"

". . . Well, now."

Her breath comes through the receiver.

"I don't believe you."

"Are you a little frightened?"

She laughs faintly.

"I'm not frightened. Should I kill that man when he gets here?"

". . . Really?"

I ring the buzzer on her building.

"Open the door. You know I can't break though the auto-lock."

The front door opens automatically. I enter the building and get on the elevator. As if confirming that I have entered, the automatic door closes, followed by the elevator door. I have no desire to turn back.

I get out on the sixth floor, where she lives, and stand before her door. I am about to ring her doorbell when, unabashedly, my hand reaches for the doorknob. It is unlocked. I grasp the cold knob and open the door, entering her apartment. She is at the end of the hallway. She is wearing a white bathrobe and looks at me with concern. As if she feels sorry for me in such a desperate state. I walk over, clasp her to me, and kiss her. Her arms embrace my neck. Her tongue thrusts inside my mouth.

". . . Did you break up with that girl?" she asks me in between kisses, her eyes still narrowly open.

"I broke up with her."

"You're lying . . . You're just ignoring her phone calls, aren't you?"

"I broke up with her."

I throw her down on the bed and kiss her again. Forcefully, I untie the sash on her bathrobe.

". . . You seem like a bad man, with that look on your face."

"I'm going to turn into a bad person, worse than you."

". . . Bad enough to kill someone? There are ways . . ."

I don't feel like talking anymore. I don't need any conversation. I kiss the nape of her neck over and over, pushing aside her bathrobe. My lips are drawn by the glimpse of her shoulders and breasts. Her scent spreads all around me. I feel the softness of her breast as my mouth touches her nipple.

"Ah . . . don't."

She strokes my hair. I kiss her again. Over and over. I take off my belt and unbutton my shirt.

". . . Wait a minute. There's something I want to show you."

Heedlessly, my lips are drawn to her body. Pushing aside her bathrobe again, I drop the unfastened sash under the bed. Her voice comes out like an exhalation as she stretches out an arm and takes out something from the shelf beside the bed.

"The photo of me, that my brother took . . . The one I told you about . . . My brother sent it to me . . ."

Her eyes are narrow as she speaks.

"The one that reveals my true nature. Look . . ."

I ignore her. I put my arms around her back and take her nipple in my mouth again.

"See . . . Ah . . . Look."

She holds the photo right in front of my eyes. My breath catches.

". . . Will you . . . save me?"

She looks at me.

". . . There's someone I want you to kill."

Archive 5

Archive 5

Your letter is really boring.

The reason why you became a member of K2. Do you think you can satisfy me with that kind of scratch? If you're going to peer inside someone's mind, you're going to have to reveal something of yourself.

From now on, I'm not going to write anything about the murders. Not until you give me something definitive about your own self. No matter how lonely I may be, I'm not going to let you talk me into going there.

You got it? Don't be so disappointed. It's your own fault anyway.

———

But then again, sitting here like this, in a prison cell and in front of a blank page, one is wont to write something. They say that death-row inmates are always writing letters. Some of them just keep writing letters addressed to no one—who knows who they're intended for. I should be happy I still have someone to write to. That's why I'm asking you. Come on, show me just what's inside your head.

———

. . . I guess I'll tell you about when I was arrested. Something different from what you want to hear about. I've been thinking I'd like to try to describe to someone how strange it was when that happened. Maybe, if it were you, you might have thought it was happening to someone else.

When they put the handcuffs on me, I thought, "They

caught me." . . . It may sound strange, but I remember feeling tremendously relieved. Like they had finally seized hold of a balloon that had been floating all over the place. Now I would no longer have to lie to anyone. Now I would no longer have to keep up with the confusion inside my mind . . . The irony is that prison is what a criminal is trying to avoid, but it is also the very thing that, at his core, he is yearning for. Here he no longer needs to go on living as an alien entity within a normally functioning society. The alien entity finds himself when he's in handcuffs. It felt like . . . an appropriate resolution to my life.

What's more . . . once I was arrested, I wouldn't be able to have a camera anymore. I wondered if I would be capable of being separated from my camera. The camera . . . Who invented such a thing? . . . What a terrifying device. Don't you think?

But people are—no, I mean I am—very selfish. I was arrested, and now that my life has been significantly restricted, after a while, I find myself wanting to be out there again. I find myself wanting to hold a camera once more. If I were to get out, I wonder if the balloon would start floating all over the place in the confines of my mind once more, and then explode again. Then I'd be arrested and relieved all over again. It's a harsh existence . . . See what I mean? Sometimes I think they should just kill me already.

I'm not doing so great today. I had thought it might relax me a bit if I wrote for a while, but the words are depressing me. Usually I can only write letters when I'm feeling calm enough.

Part of my obsession with cameras is that, even though I'm a criminal, there are still people who think the photographs I took mean something. But then, my photos . . . No, I think it would make you happy to read this so I won't write it. I'll just say that, lately, there's one thing I can't stop thinking about. It's . . . well, I wonder why the hell was I born?

———

. . . A pretty random tangent, I guess. But this is your fault. Because you refuse to reveal yourself.

By the way, recently someone else has emerged who wants to write a book about me. He's already come to visit me twice at the prison. We talked through the acrylic glass. And you haven't even come to see me once.

Just like you, he has a habit of jumping the gun with his questions, and he seems kind of unreliable, but apparently my sister has taken a liking to him. I don't know what she finds appealing about a wobbler like him . . . but he must have some redeeming qualities.

And what about you? Were you really a member of K2? Are you really trying to write a book about me? I don't know the first thing about you from your letters. I don't know what you look like. Or even what your voice sounds like. Because you've made no effort at all to come visit me.

So I need to ask you this fundamental question: *Just who the hell are you?*

10

THIN THREADS OF rain are soaking the ground, as though it doesn't really matter if it falls or not.

Usually I don't care if I get wet but I put up my umbrella. I am on my way to meet someone. It makes people uncomfortable when you show up sopping wet.

I had fled back home from Akari Kiharazaka's apartment. I had left her like that, halfway out of her bathrobe. I am a mess. In a bad way. My head is throbbing, and I futilely clench my molars together. It isn't as if that is going to make my headache go away.

Sensing something, I turn around to see a cat behind me. The cat is black, the area around its belly helplessly white. For some reason the cat has been following close behind me. Like it is checking to see what my fate is. As I hold up my umbrella, my bag feels heavy. I am aware of the recorder and notebook and stationery I am carrying. I still cannot bring myself to write a single letter to Yudai Kiharazaka. He seems to expect me to open up to him in a letter, but I can't figure out how to write to him. I even have envelopes with me. And of course pens too. Maybe, once I start writing, the words will come to me. I have still only met him twice.

I can see a concrete wall. The high enclosure conceals an old mansion. There are numerous trees. Inside the grounds, the house surrounded by that wall seems familiar for some reason.

I ring the doorbell. I hear a woman's voice, and a moment later the door opens. A still youthful woman comes to greet me. Smiling, she guides me through a large garden.

"We've been expecting you."

These words are spoken by a man who has been crouching in the garden. He is the doll creator, Suzuki. He is wearing the white sweat suit that is his work clothes. The color is different, but it resembles the outfit that I had seen Yudai Kiharazaka wearing.

"I thought it was about time you came around. You're writing a book about Kiharazaka, are you?"

He smiles as he speaks. The woman is also smiling as she looks at me. I sense something behind me, and turn around to see the same cat from before. It approaches the doll creator and then rolls over on the ground. It must be Suzuki's cat. As I look closer, I see it is wearing a collar.

". . . Yes. I'm a mess. I, uh . . ."

"You're in over your head?"

"I am."

". . . I see," he says with concern in his amiable voice. I wonder how old he is. I had thought he was in his forties, but he had looked younger when I saw him outside of his home.

"Please come inside. I'm not working today."

The woman opens the front door and leads me inside. We walk down a hallway and come into a familiar spacious tatami room. My breath catches. There are countless dolls, all wearing different clothes. They seem utterly alive. Of course, I know very well that they aren't alive but, I can't help thinking, they are by no means dead either. Although my brain registers them as human, a part of me still seems aware that they definitely are not. The vivid gazes of the various dolls are looking in every direction. My eyes lock with one of them. My heart starts to race a little. If I look at them from even a slightly different angle, each of the dolls' expressions seems completely changed.

". . . Lately, I haven't been able to make any for pleasure. I've been too busy."

"You have many commissions?"

"Yes. Maybe it's the times we live in. There are a lot of requests for ones modeled on living people."

The doll creator smiles when he says this. His eyes are extremely narrow, his skin pale. His long hair has a gentle wave and is neatly arranged.

"I heard that used to be taboo."

"Yes. But if they keep asking for it . . ."

"I also heard that one doll told the guy to kill the real woman she was based on."

Suzuki looks at me with pity when I say this. Even though he is the one who has created such a doll.

"What a shame. Really, such a shame. But I am simply the doll maker. All I'm doing is actualizing people's desires. Once actualized, certain things also become apparent."

I drink the tea that the woman has prepared and brought out. The doll creator is sitting directly on the tatami, so I sit down myself. Right in front of the dolls. At some point the woman has disappeared.

"Is she . . . ?"

"Oh, she's a doll."

". . . What?"

"Ha ha ha, it's a joke." The doll creator laughs with real delight. "No, she is a sort of apprentice. She came to me so that I could make one of her husband who passed away. She sleeps with me regularly but her heart still completely belongs to her husband."

". . . And what about your heart?"

"My heart?"

Suzuki looks at me.

". . . I have no such thing."

The cat from earlier comes into the room. It prowls around us, then seems to lose interest and vanishes again. I sip the tea that the woman has made, and Suzuki does the same. After a while, he smiles.

"That's a lie. I was joking with you again. She's only sleeping with me so that I'll make her a doll. A doll has to be a copied after a person. It shouldn't be copied after a doll. That's why I need to have contact with people."

"You . . ."

"Ha ha ha, you're not here to talk about me, are you? But rather about Kiharazaka."

He looks at me through his narrow eyes.

"He was a top-notch photographer. But unfortunately . . . he tried to go beyond that. Perhaps what he sought to be doesn't even exist. Take a look over there."

I let my gaze follow Suzuki's hand. At one side of the room, past all the other dolls, there is one that appears to be in the process of being made. It has no hair, its flesh-colored body is exposed, it isn't wearing any clothes. Neither the face nor the body have the texture of real skin.

"That doll does not yet have any life in her. The doll does not resemble anyone, or have any distinctive characteristics. That's the one—the one that appears in the background of his photo, *Butterflies*."

". . . What?"

" His desires were all imitations of someone else. That is to say, there was nothing inside him."

The doll creator is still looking at me.

"We did an experiment, when it was just me and him. He asked me to create what would be his ideal woman, so I picked up a pencil and sketched it out. But no matter what, the face of the woman he described always resembled someone else. His sister or his mother, a celebrity, the waitress he had just seen . . . Our predilections—what we call our desires—I guess that's just how they work. But then, seeing what I had inadvertently drawn, I decided to test him. I said, 'I prefer this kind of woman.' And then he too gradually took a liking to the same things. After a while he started saying,

with considerable enthusiasm, Make me a doll like this . . .
Then, in the midst of it all, he realized what had happened
and he went quiet."

Suzuki draws in a quick breath, and calmly continues.

"What first got him interested in cameras was a commercial he saw with a friend. In the commercial, a cool-looking
guy was using a camera in a cool way. As they were watching,
Kiharazaka's friend beside him said, 'Sure would be nice.' With
a look of envy, he had said, 'It sure would be nice to have that.'
At that moment, Kiharazaka felt just the slightest desire for
the camera. And from then on, he told me, his desire for the
camera grew stronger and stronger."

"That's just . . ."

"There is nothing inside him. He fell in love with his
sister because he saw a movie about incest. And because the
woman who starred in it was very beautiful and sexy. What's
more, he told me, the guy he saw the movie with had joked
about how nice it would be to have a gorgeous sister like
that. So even though it got started that way—or no, precisely
because it started that way—from then on, little by little, his
desire was heightened, until he was pathologically obsessed.
It's his attempt to turn his own desire, which is an imitation
of someone else's desire, into the real thing."

The doll creator looks down for a moment, then back
at me.

"Then, he killed two women. I bear some of the responsibility for that . . . Because of a conversation we had."

". . . A conversation?"

"A conversation about another doll maker I admire. Today, I will tell you everything I know."

The rain is falling outside.

"Are you familiar with the conflict known as the Onin War, which occurred during the last years of the Muromachi shogunate? It was a terrible period, a time when the shogunate lost its ability to function, causing samurai throughout the various regions to form their own armies, and the entire country devolved into an internecine war. No one knew who they were battling against or even for what purpose, different conflicts broke out simultaneously—it was an era of unprecedented madness in Japan's history. Afterward we entered into what's known as the Warring States Period, but what I want to talk about now is a gifted creator of wind-up dolls who lived during the era of that Onin War. That is to say . . . This is a story about how, in a time of great confusion, one man transcended death."

He smiles.

"This doll maker was known—even more than for his art—for the skill with which he used the color red. Every wind-up doll that he had made up to that point had worn a magnificent vermilion kimono. The doll maker's wife was in poor health. She was bedridden practically all the time, and the doll maker had always taken care of her. He loved his wife very much. But his love for her was intense. And in his passion for her, well, their sex practically destroyed his frail wife. The doll maker had an idea. Could he make a doll of his wife? But if he made a doll of a living person, that person would die. That's what he believed. However, one day, his wife asked him to make a doll of herself. I'm going to die soon, she said. I will only become frailer. I want you to make a doll of me while I'm still pretty. Hearing her words, the doll maker started to produce a wife doll."

It is still raining outside. I am listening closely to his story, to his soft voice.

"That alone makes this a sad and touching story. Most people can only tolerate it up to this point . . . You probably already know what happens. Before long, as the doll maker immersed himself in the production of his wife doll, he started to lose his mind. The doll's beauty began to exceed that of his wife. As the doll neared completion, his wife's physical condition deteriorated. It was like the doll was extracting her life force. What's more, his chisel had slipped several times during the frequent earthquakes, or the edge of the plane had happened to shave marks into the wood, but these mistakes had, on the contrary, brought out the doll's unexpected beauty. Rather, through a series of unintended coincidences, the doll had exceeded the doll creator's abilities, as if it were using a divine power—no, the power of the earth, the earth that was soaked with the blood of so many killed in the war—and had become something that transcended human understanding . . . The wife was jealous. That is, the wife was jealous of herself—she experienced jealousy of her own more beautiful self. The doll maker devoted himself to the production of the doll and stopped paying attention to his wife. Early in the morning, all day long, and into the night, the sound of his chisel carving away at the doll echoed from his house . . . Later, the doll maker was discovered to be living with both the red wife doll and the skeletal corpse of his actual wife, months after her death."

Little by little, the temperature in the room was growing chilly.

"But there was one thing that the wife managed to do before she died. Abandoning the effort to tear her husband away from the doll, the wife could only pray for his future destruction, now that he had become the object of her inevitable enmity. On the verge of death, she suddenly found the strength to stand up. She pulled herself up behind her husband, who would no longer have anything to do with her, immersed as he was in the creation of the doll. And she put a curse on her husband: 'You will never again be able to live with anyone except this doll.' The wife coughed up blood on the doll. This cough was fatal, her last. The doll maker stared at the blood-stained doll. At its overwhelming beauty. This was exactly the shade of red that he had been seeking—the red that a person spews out as they are dying. The doll, her skin stained blood red, had taken on a maddening beauty. From that day forward, the doll maker became oblivious to all other women. Even if he attempted to demonstrate some kind of interest, he was simply unable to. As for flesh-and-blood humans, no one existed in this world beside the doll. And that was not all. The doll maker was no longer able to produce any other work, either. Because he could never attain that same shade of red. He would never again have access to the blood coughed up by his beloved wife. The doll maker had been drawn in by the totality of the doll's beauty, born of a series of coincidences and further enhanced by his wife's crimson blood. The doll maker finally died of madness. These were his last words, and herein lies the problem: 'Once my wife died the doll grew even more beautiful.'"

Suzuki suddenly stands up and approaches his own doll creations. He strokes their hair impassively.

"The doll was kept at a temple for a while, but ultimately it was disposed of. Because *it should never have existed* in the first place. Not only the doll's creator, but any man who took one look at the doll was rendered impotent. Whenever they tried to make love to a woman, that red doll would appear before them as a vision. And the doll's expression . . . she seemed to be faintly smiling. But none of them could tell just what kind of smile it was—or what kind of smile it wasn't. Just like the Mona Lisa's smile. Except where the Mona Lisa's smile conveys the beauty of art to those who view it, this doll's smile gave rise to nothing but madness. Forever bewildered by what was behind her smile, these men were filled with agony and vertigo. In both cases, the painting and the doll, the smile appears to be that of a real person. It's a kind of artifice; nevertheless, human perception recognizes it as a 'smile.' Why does that happen, when it comes to perception? In any case, unable to determine just what kind of smile it was, the men's confusion deepened until it seemed to drive them crazy . . . Does this sort of thing happen to other creatures? If you were to show a dog a painting of a dog, I wonder by just which qualities in the painting would the dog recognize another dog?"

Suzuki looks at me pensively.

"Well, I . . . I wanted to make a doll like the one that doll creator had made. Something that shouldn't be made. Something that shouldn't exist . . . You must think I'm mad. It doesn't matter. My life is already over, to a certain extent. But I told Kiharazaka about all of this. I can't help thinking that the two murders were the results of that conversation."

"But . . . he also talked to Saito."

"Saito? You mean that stalker guy?"

"Yes. So . . ."

"That's interesting. So I wasn't the only one who talked to him about things they shouldn't have. Wouldn't two conversations be enough to have an impact on him? And also, I'm the one who made Saito's doll in the first place. That makes me the root of all his evils."

"Do you really think so?"

"What?"

"I mean . . ."

I hold my tongue. I want to say something, but I can't find the words.

It is raining heavily now. The doll maker parts the curtain slightly and is facing outside but his eyes don't seem focused on anything. I reach for my cup only to realize that it is empty. The doll maker looks at me again pensively.

"Well, the first victim, Akiko Yoshimoto, burned to death. It was deemed an accidental fire, because Kiharazaka suffered major burns as well, and his studio was completely destroyed. But, I knew it then. That it hadn't actually been an accident."

". . . What do you mean?"

"I saw the photographs he took."

Suzuki looks directly at me with his narrow eyes. My heart starts to race.

"Photographs of Akiko Yoshimoto, in the raging fire. Are you familiar with the story, 'Hell Screen'?"

". . . Yes. By Ryunosuke Akutagawa."

"That's right. Kiharazaka was morbidly fascinated by that story. There must have been somebody who had casually recommended it to him . . . He set fire to his lover, and then took photographs of her. But he didn't show them to anyone. Of course not. If such photos existed, they would find out what he had done. After all."

The doll maker draws in a quick breath.

"*He thought they would become more beautiful—the photos he took of her—if she were to die*. Once the real her was dead. Like Saito's doll. Like that doll made by the doll maker during the Onin War. Kiharazaka tried to create art that he shouldn't have. Just like me. He ventured into territory where he didn't belong. Akiko was visually impaired. To do such a thing to a woman like that. And in imitation of someone else."

". . . Ryunosuke Akutagawa's 'Hell Screen' is based on *The Tale of Uji Shui* and the *Kokon Chomon*, isn't it?"

"Yes. The work has a cultural lineage. That's what he was trying to do with his photographs. But it led him to a strange question. Which photos were actually more beautiful—the photos of his lover on fire? Or did the photos he had already taken of her gain in beauty, now that she was dead?"

He shows me several photographs. I reach my hand out to them. My fingers are trembling slightly.

The first one is a photograph of Akiko Yoshimoto on fire.

Her eyes are closed as she is engulfed by intense flames. The second one is a photograph of the interior of the room, engulfed by the same inferno. The third one is a photograph of Akiko Yoshimoto, the victim, taken when she was alive. She is in the studio, seated in a chair, her eyes closed, a faint smile on her lips. There are also photographs of the other victim, Yuriko Kobayashi. One photo of her engulfed in flames, another of the room as it looked at the time, of the walls and equipment about to collapse. There are numerous other photographs as well. Of the flames, of the women as they are burning, of the studio on fire.

But, I think to myself. But . . .

"Do you see? They're quite terrifying, aren't they? *This is his failure. He photographed women to their death.* What's more, his photos of them aren't even particularly powerful. He was in the midst of a slump at the time. He took these photos in an attempt to break out of his slump. I say slump, but it's not what an ordinary photographer would consider a slump. What I mean by slump is, well, ruin. And by ruining himself, it's not just that he would be rendered incompetent—he would have driven himself mad in the process, creating photographs that should never have existed. But he failed. There have been whispers from various quarters about the mystery of why, if he went to the trouble of burning these two women, did he not take any photographs, but the reason is simple. He did take photographs, and he failed. He couldn't show them to anyone. He asked me to keep them to myself."

"You mean that's why he tried again? With the second woman?"

"That's right. The second victim, Yuriko Kobayashi, who was working for him as a model, was killed in exactly the same way. As a result, the true facts of all that happened were brought to light. He will always be one to lie about everything, but that is the whole truth. Then again, there was more to it than just that. Kiharazaka's sister is probably a lesbian." The doll maker's voice lowers another register.

"What?"

"You should back out of this. Coincidentally, I was thinking of getting out of it myself. There are things here that even I don't understand. No matter how obsessed he was with photography, for his madness to have compelled him to go so far as murder—something else must have been at play. *Do you really think that a person could murder someone, purely for the sake of art?* There must be something that fostered his madness to such a point. There's a more brutal madness to this than two simple murders. Why Akari made me such an offer . . . Look closely at this. You may not have noticed it."

Suzuki points to one of the dolls among the many behind him. My heart begins to race.

(11)

THE HUGE CLOCK hanging on the wall seems to have stopped moving.

"I think I want to quit working on this project."

The moment I say it, I feel a small pang of regret, along with a calm sense of release. My editor gazes across at me, looking slightly dazed.

"Why . . . ?"

". . . It's too much for me. I'm sorry."

"I want you to explain to me, specifically. What happened?"

We are at my editor's apartment. I stare at the glass of whiskey on the table. My editor is staring at the same thing. He lights a cigarette. I remain silent.

". . . You mean, you're in over your head?"

I look at the unmoving clock on the wall. It seems disproportionately large for the room. He opens his mouth to speak.

"Have you read Truman Capote's *In Cold Blood*?"

". . . I have."

"After he completed his nonfiction novel, he couldn't write another decent piece of work. His spirit was broken. Then again, at least he did finish that book."

Akari Kiharazaka had said something very similar to me. My heart starts to race. My editor raises his voice slightly.

"Sure, the way that I do things may be relentless. Some have even called me pathological because I always push a writer beyond the limits of his abilities. And as a result, some writers' spirits have broken. But I just want to make a good book. That's all. It may sound callous, but I'm not thinking about the writer. The only thing I care about it is the work."

"I understand that."

"Really?"

The editor looks me straight in the eyes.

"Capote managed to write his all. He put his heart and soul into it. And you—you're going to give up at this point?"

He still isn't finished with what he has to say.

"It's frustrating. I'm disappointed to hear your position. It sounds like you're putting your personal life above your own work. Get out of here."

He takes another drag from his cigarette.

"Don't bother sending me your expenses. This will be a major loss for us. And I don't want to deal with you anymore."

Archive 6

A woman with a towel wrapped around her face is being embraced by a man.

The woman's pleasure is conveyed through her body's response. She gently caresses the man's face as his tongue trails between her breasts. The man also has a towel wrapped around his face, but his eyes and mouth are visible.

The man slowly enters the woman. She arches her back, spreading her legs wide and then coiling them around his waist, squeezing. The man thrusts his hips, and the woman takes him in. There is no sound on this picture.

Staying inside her, the man lies down on the bed so that the woman is on top of him. The woman moves her hips vigorously. She is completely absorbed in the act, but every so often, the man steals a glance in the direction of the camera as if confirming its location.

The man is filming the encounter with a hidden camera. The woman is unaware.

The man pulls away, flips the woman onto all fours, and enters her from behind. No passive participant, the woman is still moving her hips like an insect in heat. The white sheets are soaked from the wetness seeping from between her legs. The man pulls out of her and even more fluid that has accumulated inside her gushes out. He looks at the camera once—as if he wants to make sure it caught the flow of her wetness on film—and then puts his sex back inside the woman. He thrusts his hips briskly. She is moving her own hips carelessly, as if nothing seems to matter.

The man is not wearing a condom. He is about to come inside the woman. It is as if he insists on pumping every last drop deep into her. The woman's body quivers as she takes it within her. She is slender, but her body brims with sensuality, suggesting she has slept with many men. The woman moves to kiss the man, and he tries to take the towel from her face. The picture abruptly ends there.

Archive 7

Essay Composition (10 years old)

I don't have a mother or father. That's why I can't write anything about my parents. I have an older sister, but if I write
about her, the teacher will tell me that I'm wrong, so instead I'll
write about the director at the institution. The director always
tells us he is our parent. But that sounds bad, and sometimes,
I think it is bad.

This one time, we were at Okawa Park, and I saw a father
and a mother and a girl, they were walking. I'd seen things
like that lots of times before. But this time was weird. This
time, I thought, I could be that girl. I thought that was weird.
If I were that girl, and somebody called me a fake, I would
probably get mad.

The girl was holding hands and walking with her mother
and father. She was smiling and wearing nice shoes. I thought
I remembered that I had made that girl cry once, but really
what happened was, she called me a fake. That's why I
thought she was lucky to be a girl, because she was the real
thing. Other girls were passing by me, and the sun was really
bright, and it was like there were traces of green everywhere
catching my eye. My eyes started to hurt, and I thought, my
eyes really hurt. It was like there were cracks—cracks in the
telephone pole, cracks in the street, cracks everywhere. The
cracks were getting bigger and bigger, and I got scared, so I

tried to close my eyes, but I couldn't, not at all. I felt like I was in the wrong place, and when I felt like that, my heart was pounding. I tried to look at the girls again. But with the traces of green and all the cracks everywhere, I couldn't really see. It felt like the cracks were all around me, and then I couldn't breath, so I tried to run, far away, so I could escape.

My friend Katani has video games, and I think he's lucky. I don't know if I'd rather be him or that girl. I wish my friends thought I was lucky.

When I told the director about this, he tried to cheer me up. The director is nice. He takes good care of me. He gave me money on New Year's. I was happy. But I didn't get as much as everyone else, so that made me a little sad. But I was still happy.

Archive 8

Archive 8

All of a sudden you want to call off the interview with me? Don't you think that's a little one-sided?

You came to see *me*. You said you were writing a book about me. To quit now is too irresponsible. I'm utterly baffled, to get this letter out of the blue. There was another person who wanted to write a book about me too (I'm sorry for not mentioning this; if you had come to see me again, I would have told you about it) but his letters suddenly stopped. I never met the guy, only got his letters, so I was feeling more inclined to trust you. Besides, my sister liked you. So what's this all about? I want you to explain it to me. Stop upsetting me like this.

You know, I'm trying to get them to go ahead and execute me. But, sometimes, I waver about it. When I hear the word "execution," I think, the sooner the better. I've got too much time. Meanwhile, there are nights when I tremble. Even though I try to keep my fear in check, I can't help it—there are times when I get scared. Of course it's my own fault. But what scares me are the things I can't do anything about. Lately I've had terrible hallucinations. There's somebody who's trying to attack me. This is the only thing I can't bear. How could someone attack me when I'm in prison? Not even my sister can save me. My sister loves me but, at the same time, she quietly hates me. I can tell. You're the only hope I have left.

Should I tell you about it? You may think I'm a coward, but maybe I should tell you about it. All right, but read carefully.

I'm not writing this to you because I don't want to be executed. I'll say it again. I'm not writing this because I don't want to be executed. It's not because I'm struggling. But, if you still have any interest in my case, would you consider contacting the media? That lawyer doesn't believe what I tell him. His entire strategy is built on me being mentally unstable. That was part of the scheme. To make me lose my mind . . . Everyone is watching me. No, that's not right. What I mean is that everyone is listening in on me, to hear what I'm doing. They're using the concrete walls and the iron doors like an eardrum. That's why, even when writing this letter, I'm doing so very quietly. I can't have them knowing what kind of letter I'm writing by the sounds I'm making. Clever, aren't I? I know what I'm doing.

From now on, I've got to write even more quietly. Without making a sound . . . All right, listen closely.

Those two murders were not my fault. The women are to blame.

Do you remember the first time we met? Remember what I said? That to me it felt like we were sitting in a cramped little room, talking face to face. Now, you and I find ourselves in that same situation again. I'm clinging to you desperately now. Do you know the story about the freelance writer who lost his mind because the condemned criminal who didn't want to die was counting on him? I am now burdening you with this. I'm not going to let you get away. There's no way I will let you escape!

About the first incident, Akiko Yoshimoto. She was beautiful. I thought I would help her, since she couldn't see. A little before I met her, I had seen a movie that was just like that. I took photographs of her to try to get close to her. So many photographs . . . But it didn't work. No matter how many photos I took, I was unable to capture a more beautiful version of her.

I thought it was the fault of the model. At that time, there were those who said I was in a slump, but that was definitely not the case. I knew I had the ability, and as long as I had a good model, I could take good photographs. I made her sit in that chair forever, and because she'd try to get away, I'd tie her legs with rope and take more photographs. She grew thin. But I had no choice. I wasn't eating myself. Don't you think it would have been strange for her to eat, so long as I wasn't eating? And the image of her in my mind required her to be thin for the photographs. I didn't think there was any need for me to feel bad about her not eating since I wasn't eating either.

Do you know the short story "Hell Screen," by Ryunosuke Akutagawa? I kept seeing it before my eyes. Her body on fire. Or to be more precise, a photograph of her body on fire. A photograph of her engulfed in flames. The color of the flames when a body burned . . . I had that vision. All that was left was for her to burn. But that wasn't my intention. I never plotted to set her alight with a candle flame. It was just there as part of the photo shoot, I didn't set her on fire deliberately. Nevertheless, there she was, burning right before my eyes. It was a phenomenon generated by my talent. I became increasingly abstracted . . . it's true, you've got to believe me. My whole studio burned down. I suffered burns myself. But it may have been lucky for me that the rope that had bound her legs also burned. That was why . . . it was possible for the fire to be ruled an accident. As might be expected, not even the guys who came to the scene and examined her burnt corpse could detect any sign of the rope. And as for photographs, there were none. Why would I have taken any? There wouldn't have been time for that! Because it was an accident. There was nothing I could have done about it.

———

About the second incident, Yuriko Kobayashi . . . That time, she was the one who got close to me. It's true. I can be pretty charming. All those things everyone said—that I followed her around like a stalker, or that I snatched her away in the blue sedan I always drove, or that I kept her in my studio against her will—those are all lies. That's the conspiracy. Do you believe the conspiracy? Are you no different from the guys who are trying to listen in on what I'm writing to you in this letter by the sound of my pen right now? That's the conspiracy. This is just between you and me, all right? I'm going to tell you a secret that's really frightening. The truth of the matter is that the prosecutor, and the judge and the jury—all of them were in on it together. They are all working together behind the scenes to have me put to death. It's true. This information is coming to you straight from the source. It doesn't matter. And as if that weren't enough, now they're trying to attack me. Can you believe it?

You know, she was always asking me to kill her. She wanted to die. You could tell just by looking at her. I felt like I could see it in her eyes, that the girl wanted someone to kill her. I'm telling you, you would know just by looking at her. She was a diabolical woman, that Yuriko. But I wasn't the one who lit the fire. From the moment I unlocked the door to the studio (I wasn't keeping her there—I was only thinking of her safety, which is why the door was locked from the outside too) I was frantic, but there was absolutely nothing I could do. Have you ever smelled the scent of a woman's burning flesh? Its sweetness is enough to make you lose control! Whenever I try to remember that moment, I get distracted, and butterflies start to flutter, right in front of my eyes. The butterflies that those guys let loose, just to disturb me. The butterflies spread out as far as I can see . . . Don't think I'm telling you this because it's convenient. This is awful for me. The photographs . . . I couldn't take any. There was no time for that.

I was arrested. The second incident, with Yuriko Kobayashi, was clearly murder, so their argument was that Akiko Yoshimoto must also have been murdered. How could the first incident be an accident if the second incident was arson, they said. But I'm not an ordinary person. I'm a genius. All kinds of things happen to geniuses. Isn't that right? And then, there was the thing they got the most upset about. That all this time I had been photographing these women—and now that I had those photographs, that must be why I didn't care whether the women themselves died.

I don't want to be executed. It's all I ever think about, but now I'm afraid of dying. Some nights I scare myself thinking about it. Most of the time, I think, I might as well die the way that I am, and I feel like I'm finally ready to die, but then suddenly, just like that, I'll be terrified. I didn't do anything, and I'm going to be put to death for a crime I did not commit. Let the media know all about this! Please. Save me from death! I know, I know, I can still file an appeal. I can file an appeal! I can appeal, and be found innocent, and then I can take the best photograph of my life. I've got talent. Next time I won't fail. Next time for sure, I won't fail. Next time, I'll show you—I'll take the best photo ever taken, a photo of a burning woman. Next time, you'll see. It will be the best photo ever taken. Don't you want to see my photo? I bet you can't wait to see it. I botched the photos last time—it was a ridiculous idea. I freaked out when they were right in front of me, burning! And even though I had set them on fire, the photos were no different from any others I'd taken! You can't be giving up on your book about me. You were joking, right? It's a joke, right? It can't be true. You can't leave me alone! My sister said I should just die. She didn't say it in so many words, but she insinuated. Why would she say that? There's something obscene about the insinuations in her letters. No—I don't want to die, I don't want to die, I don't want to die, I don't want to die. I won't let you get away. There's no way I'll let you escape. You're going to save me. Come and see me. I'm begging you. You're going to save me before they attack me. Come see me. Come see me. Come see me. Come see me. Come see me . . .

But . . . what do you think? An ordinary woman dies—just what does that mean?

Archive 9

Yuriko Kobayashi's Twitter account, February 11 to February 18.

> **Yuyuko**, yuyurin1121.
> I like reading, movies, and shopping. I do a little modeling.

February 11, 2:12pm

Going shopping today (^_^) Maybe I'll buy a bag!!

February 11, 7:02pm

About to eat eel over rice, my favorite (^_^)

February 11, 7:51pm

Yummmy!!!

February 12, 1:46am

Can't sleep . . . and I have to get up early tomorrow. I'm
screwed (T_T)

February 12, 4:01pm

Got a job (O.O) With a famous photographer (O.O)

February 12, 11:08pm

Thanks everyone!!

February 12, 11:59pm

I'll do my best (>.<)

February 13, 2:12pm

I feel like I have so much support in my life (-_-:) Having a
late lunch with a friend (^_^)

February 17, 3:13pm

Actually, might not be exactly what I thought (-_-:)

February 17, 3:51pm

I'm not upset about it

February 17, 4:03pm

I'll be fine (^_^)

February 17, 4:23pm

Matsuko, you're so funny

February 18, 2:12pm

Shopping!!

(Posts end here abruptly. No further updates.)

Notes from Yuriko Kobayashi
(Personal diary, daily entries from New Year's Day to February 17, blank from February 18, starts again from February 25)

February 25

Just smile. As long as I smile, I'll be fine.

February 26

Don't get upset. Don't even think about it.

February 27

Toshiyuki, I'm sorry. I may already be dead. But I'll never forget you, Toshiyuki. I'm afraid. Help me, I'm scared.

February 28

I had no choice but to sleep with him. It's probably my fault. I'm sorry. I'm really sorry. I was frightened. Most of all, I didn't want him to hit me. It hurt really bad. It's probably my fault. I'm the one who's to blame. I'm so mad at myself. Help me. Help me, help me.

February 29

Help me

March 1

Help me   Help me   Help me

March 2

Help me   I can't stand it. I can't stand it. I can't stand it.

March 5

I don't want to die in a place like this. I don't want to die in a place like this. What are photos about anyway? What do you think life is about? What do you think it is to be a woman? I don't want to die in a place like this. I don't want to die in a place like this. I want to see my friends. I want to go places. I want to live. I want to live. I want to live. However this turns out, I want to live. Toshiyuki, you probably never want to see me again, but I want to live. Toshiyuki, I love you.

March 6

My body feels heavy. It hurts. It hurts.   Help me.

March 7

(Handwriting illegible)

March 9

(Handwriting illegible)

Folded note (found with diary)

March 18

If you're reading this, please notify the police. My name is Yuriko Kobayashi, and I'm being held captive in this house. My captor is a photographer named Yudai Kiharazaka. Please help me. He's going to kill me soon.

Folded note (found with diary)

March 29

If you're reading this, please notify the police.

My name is Yuriko Kobayashi, and I live in apartment 408 of the Alude Mansion, my address is 2-2-19 Kamogawa-cho, Nerima-ku. I'm being held captive by a photographer named Yudai Kiharazaka. My legs are tied to a pillar and I can't move. I haven't eaten anything for days.

I'm in a small blue building like a shed. If you happened to find this note somewhere away from where I am, you may not see this building anywhere nearby. He drives a blue car. His name is Yudai Kiharazaka. He's thin, he has long hair, and a mole on his cheek.

Please help me. Please notify the police. I'm enclosing a button from my clothing and a lock of my hair. The button is

from a favorite shirt, and one of my friends will recognize it. As
for my hair, most of it has been burned, and I hardly have any
left. He's going to kill me soon. But I want to live. I want to live.
Please help me. Please help me. Please help me.

(Her death occurred the day after this last note was dated. Twelve notes like this were found beneath the window. Some were wet, others were burned.)

Archive 10

Yuriko Kobayashi is sitting on a diagonal sofa.

She is in Yudai Kiharazaka's studio. With a frightened look, Kobayashi touches the hem of her skirt. There is a camera in front of her, a stationary camera mounted on a stand. Behind her there is a huge light reflector. On screen, she and the camera she is facing are seen from the right.

Looking even more frightened, she starts to touch the ends of her hair. She isn't wearing any makeup, even though in a corner of the room there is a makeup vanity for her. It is gothic in style, likely expensive, and looks to be quite old. Kobayashi stands up, then, seeming at her wit's end, she sits back down on the sofa. She looks at what is around her. Her eyes still look frightened.

Suddenly, the door behind the camera in front of her opens. A man enters. He is dragging a trunk. Seeing him with the trunk, her face contorts with even more fear. The man stands in front of the stationary camera, peering through the viewfinder as if he is checking the composition. He smiles cruelly. She says something, over and over again. Her mouth grows wider as she speaks, as if she is raising her voice. She looks like she is venting her anger. There is no sound on this picture.

The man crouches down and opens the trunk. It is massive. There is a woman inside. It is Kiharazaka's sister.

When Yuriko Kobayashi sees her, she starts to say something to the man. She looks relieved. She and the man take Akari out of the trunk. Akari seems to be in a very deep sleep.

Yuriko Kobayashi takes off her clothes, removing even her underwear, and then she dresses the naked Akari in her underwear and clothes. She takes another set of clothes from the man and puts them on. Kobayashi puts her own ring on Akari's finger. The diagonal sofa is long enough for someone to sleep on. The two of them cover Akari's face with a towel and lay her down on the sofa, placing a cloth over her body. They leave only her arms hanging limply outside of the cloth. They douse her with kerosene, much more than one would have thought necessary, and with some other kind of chemical. They also douse the sofa, as well as the rug under the sofa.

Yuriko Kobayashi looks like she isn't entirely over her fear. Both she and the man turn toward the door at the same time. Using the chair beside her, Yuriko Kobayashi exits the room by climbing through a window that opens easily. The man strikes a match and tosses it in Akari's direction. The cloth laid on top of Akari catches fire, little by little by little. The man stands there for a moment, then steps up onto the chair and climbs through the window. As he goes, he kicks over the chair, then hurriedly closes the window from the outside. Akari is left alone in the room, slowly burning, her right arm hanging limply off the sofa.

The door opens. A different man enters. Stunned, he looks at the fire burning before him. The flames grow steadily more intense. The man keeps standing there. He begins to sweat

profusely. He starts to tremble, as if he is having convulsions.
Smoke gushes forth, and the sofa is engulfed as the fire rages.
Suddenly, the man lunges at the stationary camera. He clicks
the shutter, over and over again. From the way his mouth is
moving, one can see he is crying out Yuriko Kobayashi's name.
Yet even as he calls her name, he continues to squeeze the
shutter as if he were obsessed. But there is no one else there
besides him and his sister.

The screen shifts to the window frame covered by the cur-
tains in the room. The building that houses the studio recedes
slowly, farther and farther away. It becomes clear that this
picture is being filmed with a small camera, through a gap in
the curtain no more than two centimeters wide. But then, as if
remembering something, the scene closes back in on the studio.
Someone's right hand comes into the picture—a man's hand.
In it he holds a bundle of notes of some kind. The hand isn't
trembling at all. He scatters the notes under the window of the
studio, and then the building again recedes from view.

The camera approaches a car. Inside it are Yuriko Kobayashi
and the first man. He hands her Yudai Kiharazaka's sister's
apartment key, her insurance card, and her pension account
book. Also doctored photographs and her diary, for practicing
her handwriting. Yuriko Kobayashi has regained her compo-
sure and is smiling at the man. From here it is impossible to see

his expression. The camera gets into the car. The door closes and the car slowly begins to drive away. The picture abruptly ends there.

Archive 11-1

I wonder how long I've been wrong.

But, when I look back on my life like this, I always get confused. Just when exactly did I screw up? Sometimes I get depressed and can't help but feel that, ultimately, it goes all the way back, and I should have just been born differently. Maybe life is just like that. Even if my life has been wrong, I'm going to wait and see what happens at the very end. Whatever I am, I'll be until the end. I guess . . .

Let's talk about us. Because there's little else in my life that has any meaning. Do you remember the first time we met? It was at the library. At a small symposium on Braille. I had never seen anyone experience someone's words so beautifully.

You accessed the words written in books through the tips of your fingers. Now and then, as your fingers slid forward, you smiled. You never believed it, but you were a very beautiful woman. At the time, you were reading *Snow,* by Orhan Pamuk. It's one of my favorite books. Back then, when I asked you what you were reading, you smiled as you replied to my question.

After that I quickly apologized. For disturbing you while you were reading, for disrupting the world of the book and rudely calling you back to this world. You gave me a puzzled look as I apologized. At that moment you . . . you were so lovely.

"I've read many books," you said to me. "I think something happens when you read—it's like the passage of your own life becomes immersed within something else. I've spent my life amidst the words of so many writers. Among well-chosen words, the various life stories, the frustrations and sorrows experienced by other people, as well as their hopes . . . I consider myself very fortunate."

I wonder if you remember the first time we kissed. It was on a bench in front of a fountain that was lit up. But it wasn't romantic at all. They were trying to conserve water so the fountain was turned off, and the bench was in disrepair. I was a little worried about people around us seeing, but you said, "It's all right, no one is looking." It was so strange. You, the blind one, seemed to know exactly what was going on around us.

"I love your book."

That's what you said to me. You meant a book that I edited, a biography of Michel Petrucciani. You told me that it was as though the letters you touched on the page were flooded with the unearthly melodies he played on the piano. I was so happy. But I had been pathologically obsessed with making the author rewrite that very passage, over and over again. It must have been tough on the author. Yet in return for all his hard work, he had been able to impress a woman as beautiful as you.

Making love with you was like a miracle to me. You had been worried about your own body, but you were really, truly beautiful. I was wild with excitement, and you were wild for me too.

"One's bigger than the other."

You said this to me sheepishly, while cupping your own breasts with your hands.

"Don't worry, everyone's are."

"Really?"

"Really, take your hands away."

"I don't want to."

"Ha ha, take them away."

I was so excited, I couldn't wait. I touched my lips to your breasts over and over again. Looking at your body, I thought to myself: What a gorgeous creature. What a gorgeous creature, right here before my very eyes. And someone this gorgeous wants to be with me. The body of the person you love is the most wonderful. And I was in love with you. From the bottom of my heart. So much that I didn't care what happened to me.

It seems like people who can't see are generally thought to be quiet and meek. But you were quite the opposite. You went everywhere. You told me you had been to Nepal, to Jamaica, to Singapore. When we went to Kyoto together and stood before the temples, you explained everything about them to me. The quality of the materials they were built with. Their shape and appearance. The expressions on the faces of the tourists who had come to see them. You even explained my own impressions to me. Listening and breathing it all in, you seemed to be comparing the knowledge you learned from books with everything around you, seeing it all recreated in the back of your mind. At the time, you wore a faint smile. I think it's possible that the temples you imagined in your mind may have been more beautiful than the real things.

You went everywhere. To concerts to hear the jazz you loved, to author readings and amusement parks, on walks to nature parks and to restaurants you had discovered in magazines. In places that aren't public institutions, there isn't any yellow tactile paving on the walkways. There you were with your walking stick, and I was right beside you, when a car rushed recklessly past us. Worried about you, I followed you wherever you went. You seemed so amused by my concern. You even made me stop when I tried to insist on walking on the street side to protect you. You laughed and said, "I'm worried about you."

One time we were having dinner at the apartment when there was a report on television about a murder. As you heard this on the news, you suddenly put down the chopsticks in your hand and touched my arm. Then you said, "I don't know what I would do if you were murdered," as if whispering to yourself.

"Here I am with you now, in this cozy apartment," you went on softly. "But if this reality were shattered by an event like that, I don't think I could go on."

I had been staring vacantly at the television. A young man had been stabbed numerous times in a robbery homicide. The amount stolen was only ¥12,000. The perpetrator had been arrested and was expressing his remorseful plea.

"If you were murdered, I would want revenge. Of course, that's not right, and if anything, I'm against the death penalty. But . . . if someone I cared about were murdered, I don't think I'd have a choice but to consider revenge first. I mean, it's not really to say whether it's right or wrong. To lose someone I loved would destroy my life, and in that state, I don't think I'd listen to anyone."

You were clasping my arm tightly, as if to assure yourself that I was still there with you. I didn't say anything at the time, but I was thinking the same thing as you.

I was at work when you were in the traffic accident. I had just left a big publishing house for a smaller one, and I was caught up in the dizzying pace. I rushed madly to the hospital, to find you there in bed, your leg suspended in traction, and you smiled at me in greeting. I was forced to face the possibility of losing you. Of you disappearing from this world. That terrified me. My entire world would become worthless. Grasping your hand—such a slender, warm hand—I could only be grateful that you were here now. Such a soft, irreplaceable thing . . . I would go on holding your hand forever.

After you left the hospital, I asked you to stay at home while I was working. But you just smiled at me and, as always, went everywhere. Sometimes when I was stressed out from work, I raised my voice at you without thinking. You looked at me with such sad eyes that I immediately apologized. But I couldn't stop myself from worrying about you.

I started leaving work as early as I could. When I'd get home and not find you there, I'd feel a slight panic. I'd call you and, ignoring your protests that you were all right, I'd drive over to get you. You kept telling me you could do things on your own. That you only get one life. That you didn't want to limit yourself. You wanted to experience it all. And that you didn't like it when I interfered too much in your life. Everything you said was true. Yet I couldn't control myself. "It's because I can't see," you said at last. "You worry about me because I can't see, don't you? In that case, maybe you ought to go after one of the other girls walking around out there."

But that's not what it was about. Of course, it's true that I had been worried about you because you couldn't see. But the problem was mine.

Six years before I met you, I was involved with someone else. I won't tell you her name, but we were very much in love. All she said was that her stomach hurt a little bit, and I started to worry and asked her to go to the hospital. When she came back from the local clinic and said that it was nothing serious, I still wondered if she was all right, and I begged her to go to a bigger hospital where she could have a more thorough examination.

She gave me a strange look but, seeing the state I was in, she acquiesced and went to another hospital. When she returned and again said it was nothing, I was assured for the time being but—that's how I always acted toward her.

If she said that she wasn't feeling well, I became overly concerned that it was really the flu. I even asked her not to ride in cars. Me, who would never go to the hospital when I was ill. I made her go to the hospital so many times. I wore her down. That was the reason she left me.

After that, I started to think that maybe I ought to just avoid falling in love with anyone. I lived my life, taking care not to let anyone get too close to me. As far as I was concerned, having someone to love was too much to deal with. I could feel a quiet madness within me. If I loved someone with all my heart, my worries became unbearable, to the point where they got the better of me. I was powerless against this anxiety. There was no way for me to ignore even the slightest little worry. But . . . then I met you.

At the time, the doctor said that you were very lucky to have only broken your leg in the accident. Often, I took off from work and watched you when you left the house. To make sure you made it back home without getting in another accident. I shadowed you. I have no doubt that when your friend happened to spot me walking behind you, she must have thought it was creepy. You were so angry with me when she told you what I was doing. You had every right to be. "Did you think that I wouldn't find out, because I can't see?" you demanded. I was impossible. For some time now, a rift had been forming between us that would be difficult to repair. I followed you everywhere you went. When a car passed too close to you, I forced the driver to stop and got into an argument, while you cried and pleaded with me to stop. I forbade you to take the stairs. Or to go out. Or even to boil water.

I took my eyes off you. *In that moment, I couldn't guarantee your safety.* Your life—and within that life, your self, which I could never quite perceive—went on, survived second after second. I don't understand why, in the face of those we love, we can only acknowledge the one part we can see. I can't help wondering about the you I couldn't see.

When you told me that you wanted to live apart for a while, my vision receded to the point where I could only see a blurry version of your face. You had grown weary of putting up with the suffering I inflicted on myself. You, who had always been so active and lively, had been negatively impacted by my stubborn persistence. You still cared for me, you said softly, but if we didn't spend some time apart, it would be bad for the both of us. With tears in your eyes, you tried to hold back your sobs. Your idea was unacceptable to me. But then again, it was also unacceptable for me to be a burden to you. From that day on, I always watched you from a distance.

The yellow tactile paving follows in a straight line from the station. When the yellow line meets the sidewalk along the main road, though, it suddenly disappears. This is your way home from the station. Every day, I was lying in wait for you as you made your way home along that yellow line. And that day, I waited all day to make sure that you were safe.

What made you notice me that time? On that day, I was sitting on a bench in the plaza in front of the station, and I saw you as you moved along the yellow line with your walking stick. I was relieved that, once again today, you were safe, and I watched for a while as you passed right by me. That was when you stopped in your tracks and turned to face me.

Was it my scent? Or was it just some sort of feeling? You were definitely aware of my presence. Of me, who was still watching you like a chaperon, even though we lived apart. Who would always follow you around. Who was unwilling to leave you. That day, your expression betrayed a trace of fear. Your face contorted, as if you were afraid of me. The next day, you did not walk along the yellow line. You chose another way, one that did not have tactile paving, a more dangerous route, in order to avoid me. So I stopped watching you.

It seemed better for me not to love anyone because I became a burden to the person I loved. I decided to throw myself into my work. To try to forget about you. I thought I could change myself. I forced myself to stifle my worries about you, trying to withstand the regular bouts of nausea that accompanied the effort. The nausea tended to well up around the same time in the evening that your traffic accident had occurred. I took time off from work and made myself go on a trip alone. Despite all this, I knew that I'd never be able to change, but it was the only thing I could do. When I returned from my trip, I was still the same, of course. But without a doubt, I knew that, at the very least, I absolutely needed to stop brooding about you. I even went to see a psychosomatic specialist, but he told me that I was "normal."

But if I stopped worrying about someone, and then if I were to lose that person, then just who exactly would be to blame? When it comes to relationships, the more I love someone, the less I know what is appropriate. I thought about quitting my job and living somewhere far from Tokyo. If I stayed close, I'd end up looking for you again. And I didn't want to frighten you any more. But, in my mind, I would never be able to move on from our time together.

It was about two weeks after I had left Tokyo and gone back to my hometown in Sendai, where I found a job as an editor at a local free paper. That's when I found out about your death.

Fire at the home studio of photographer Yudai Kiharazaka. Female model dies. It was an article that I just happened to read in the newspaper. The moment I saw your name written there in small print, my heart started to pound, then it was helplessly racing and, the next thing I knew, my colleagues were holding me up. You were dead . . . ? How could that be . . . ? A photographer's model . . . ? The feel of my colleagues' hands touching me suddenly made me sick. They felt like the hands of strangers. I was aware of the many fingers of my colleagues' hands. I didn't want anyone touching me. I shook free, stood up, and went to the bathroom, where I threw up. You were dead? My vision narrowed—all I could see was a tiny portion of tiled floor around the toilet. I quit my job right on the spot. I know it was unfair to my colleagues, but at the time, I couldn't think of anything else besides you.

From there, although it seems strange even to me—since I had been drinking very heavily and, in my crazed state, didn't want to cause trouble for anyone on the road—I took the bullet train. For some reason I put on a suit first. Oddly, it made me feel like I was standing up straighter. And then on the train, even though I already had several coffees that I hadn't drunk lined up on the table in front of me, I kept ordering more from the vendor girl while people eyed me curiously.

When I got back to Tokyo, I didn't go to the police to request the details, or give my name as a person involved. I was trying to keep my presence a secret, as much as possible. Probably by that time, something had already taken root in my mind. I met up with my former colleagues, reporters for a weekly magazine, and asked for the details about the incident.

Both the police and the media regarded it as an "accident." Kiharazaka had been taking photographs, with you as the model, and at one point he had taken a break and gone into another room where he was fixing something to drink. While he was in there, a candle that was being used as a photo prop fell over, setting fire to a rug that was also being used in the shoot, and the fire then spread to the paint. Being visually impaired, you were unable to flee and inhaled the smoke. At the time of the accident, Kiharazaka had suffered burns trying to rescue you, and was still screaming when he was taken to the hospital. But, I thought to myself, was that what actually happened? Really?

I started watching Kiharazaka. I shadowed him, planting myself outside his house when he was home and keeping watch. The studio where the fire occurred was on the same property as his home, and it was left in its burned out state. His new studio was housed in a crude looking shed-like building. He definitely looked worn out. Was it really an accident? I didn't know what kind of relationship had developed between you and him, but if you were lovers then he would have been a brokenhearted man, just like me. In the midst of my grief, this humanized him to me. Without a doubt, he had been careless, but I too had once almost lost you in a traffic accident. And then, *because I was trying to straighten myself out*, I had let you out of my sight, and I had let you die. I thought about meeting with him. I was tormented. Unsure of what to do, I lapsed back into old habits, and spent my time keeping watch at Kiharazaka's house. I also ordered all sorts of back issues of magazines to see his photographs. Most of the subjects in his work were shot at quite close range, and his meticulous fixation on details was apparent, yet I didn't think he seemed crazy enough to kill someone.

It was around this time when I heard the rumors about the doll creator. Living with a doll . . . I couldn't imagine it, but I thought I'd go to see him, just to hear what he had to say. I must have been fascinated by the fact that some people even started to hear their doll's voice. When I think about the condition I was in at the time, hearing voices didn't seem like a strange phenomenon at all. I wanted to hear your voice again. I thought that meant I was crazy but it didn't matter. Maybe I wanted to retreat into madness in order to escape this world.

The man who greeted me was much cheerier than I expected. This was the doll creator, Suzuki. When I nervously showed him a photo of you, his expression changed. He looked at me calmly and asked, "What kind of relationship did you have with this woman?"

". . . I dated her a long time ago."

When I said this, he gazed at me even more steadily. Then he silently got up from his seat and took down an envelope from a shelf.

"These are horrible photographs. Are you prepared to see them?"

Not knowing what they were, I nodded automatically, and the photos were placed in front of me. Photos of you, on fire. Photos of you, engulfed in flames.

My vision narrowed, and it took me some time to realize that the sensation I felt was nausea. Suzuki the doll creator started speaking again.

"The fact is, Kiharazaka and I are close. He said that he hadn't taken any photographs, but the truth is that he did. He couldn't show them to anyone, nor could he keep them, so he asked me to hold them for him. He said that an artist like me was the only person in the world he could trust, and he insisted that I absolutely couldn't show them to anyone. Seeing these photos, I didn't know what to do. I don't care much for the police. But I couldn't just keep them a secret like this either. They were proof that he murdered her."

He was speaking very deliberately, as if choosing every word.

"I was terribly disturbed, but . . . I will entrust these photographs to you. To your own discretion."

However, something seemed strange to me. Something about the photographs. Having worked as an editor, I happened to know a lot about photography. I took the photographs from Suzuki and brought them to a photographer I knew. A few days later, he told me he was of the same opinion. He agreed that these were composites.

The shot of your face on fire was a composite photograph. As well as the one of you being consumed by the flames. To be sure, twenty-one of the photographs were not composites. Among those were two shots of you, with your legs bound and looking very thin, sleeping on top of a pedestal. There were no flames in either photo, or any sign of fire. The remaining nineteen photos were of flames. But they were all taken from a distance.

If Kiharazaka had burned you to death, in order to photograph the scene in the manner of Ryunosuke Akutagawa's "Hell Screen," wouldn't he have persisted in following through completely, as shown in the composites? If he were going to burn you that way, there would be no point in photographing it as a long shot. By now I've seen nearly all of his photographs. These long-shot photographs—all of the ones that were the real thing and not composites—didn't seem like his work at all.

I wondered if the truth was something else. Judging from the photos, he had been holding you captive. Forcing you to sleep and binding your legs, not letting you move around. That would fit with what the article said, that a candle being used as some kind of prop had fallen over and started the fire. When he realized it, he had hurriedly clicked away with his camera, rather than try to rescue you. Judging by the layout of the non-composite photos, he could have saved you before the flames overtook you. You would probably still have suffered burns all over your body, but judging from these photos, it definitely seems possible that he could have dragged you out of the flames—*had he not stopped to take nineteen photographs*. In what appears to be the last photo he actually shot, you are already completely immersed in flames.

Yet none of these photographs are successful. Not the least bit stimulating to the viewer—they are no more than mediocre. I can't help but think that the composition of the close-ups in the composite photographs was motivated by his regret—that these were the photographs he had really wanted to capture.

I tried to verify my hypothesis. I thought if I went to see Kiharazaka, though, I'd end up killing him. So I met with his sister. She was living on her own in Ueno, off an inheritance from her grandfather.

After hearing what I had to say, she bowed deeply. Then she told me that what I had said was probably correct. That her brother may not be a respectable fellow, but he didn't have the nerve to kill someone. That he may not have killed you directly himself, but morally, he bore an immense responsibility in your death. And that he now seemed destroyed. Then she said, as for what to do with these photographs, that of course she would leave it up to me. She was crying the whole time.

To have a brother like that, one whom she used to love . . .

Kiharazaka's sister Akari seemed weary of her life, a woman beset by countless miseries. When I asked her, she said that she had lost two people dear to her, men with whom she had been in love.

I was at a loss. If I brought the photographs to the police, Yudai Kiharazaka would be charged with one crime or another. But he wouldn't be sentenced to death. The murder wasn't pre-meditated, and there was only one victim. Even though he'd go to prison, he'd be out again in a few years. Yet as far as society was concerned, he'd have paid for his crime.

Akari asked me to see her again. She said it might not be her place to say such a thing, but she thought that being with me seemed to make her feel a little better. I started seeing her often after that, all the while worrying about what I should do next. I told her about my relationship with you. She told me about how she had lost one of the men who had been dear to her. A traffic accident, she said. She cried quietly while she told the story.

Some time after I first met Akari, we were just leaving each other at a coffee shop when someone called out to me from behind. The man looked terribly sad. He was around the same age as me, about thirty-five or thirty-six, and he wore an expensive suit.

"We need to talk," He said to me abruptly.

". . . You and me? What for?"

"It's about Akari Kiharazaka . . . Please excuse me, but I know all about you."

Archive 11-2

Reluctantly, I accompanied this man back into the coffee shop where I had just been with Akari. The coffee that he ordered arrived, and as soon as the waitress walked away, he slid aside the gaudy wristwatch he was wearing. Underneath was a large gash. A suicide scar.

"You should stay away from her. You'll end up like me."

"What do you mean?"

"Please excuse me . . . You are contemplating avenging the death of Ms. Yoshimoto. But right now you're worried about the best way to do so. Am I wrong?"

"How do you . . . ?"

He was a lawyer. Long ago, he said, his life had been destroyed by Akari Kiharazaka. He seemed like a creepy guy. I even resented him for trying to help me. When it comes to love, there's no such thing as fair. Akari had told me herself that she had a number of enemies. That she was apt to be misunderstood. There had been times, it was true, when I had detected a creepy quality in her laugh, as it rose to an almost unconscious cackle. But she wasn't the ruthless woman the lawyer made her out to be. He was probably stalking her. I managed to get out of there without antagonizing him. I didn't know what he might do to me if he thought I was her boyfriend.

After that I met up with Akari in coffee shops a number of times. When I saw the lawyer from afar, we'd switch locations. Then I went to her apartment and . . . I slept with her. I was reassuring her as she cried inconsolably, only to find that I myself was also in need of comforting. The world without you can be a harsh place—it's unbearable to live on, just going through the motions. I felt guilty about sleeping with someone I didn't even love, but the two of us each needed the other to lick our wounds. At least, that's what I told myself.

But I was in for a surprise. I guess I still didn't realize people could be so unpredictable. After I came inside her, I pulled away and, in the afterglow, I was stroking her hair when she ducked her head and began to quiver. Wondering what was wrong, I tried to peer at her face and was shocked to see that she was laughing. Convulsively. Her face turning painfully red.

"Oh, it's too much, I can't take it . . . I mean, you took such a long time before you fucked me."

After sex, the expression of her face seemed like it was shifting, little by little. Her attitude toward me, even the way she talked—everything was different.

"I've never been with a guy who pays so much attention when he's fucking a woman. Ah, but what does it matter. Since I set you up like that."

She said this and once again burst into silent mirth.

Everyone lies. But amid the overwhelming monotony of the everyday, it's the rare individual who enjoys lying, who indulges and revels in it, who relishes treating others with malice.

"Oh, how strange. Seriously, you really are a simpleton. When I see a guy like you, it makes my skin crawl."

I looked at her, stunned.

"I'll tell you something. That girl, Akiko Yoshimoto . . . I'm the one who kidnapped her."

". . . What?"

"Do you think a woman who's that cautious would give in to a man's advances? I snatched her away in a car. At my brother's request."

She was still laughing.

"Do you know Greek mythology? Just as Oedipus unknowingly kills his own father, just as Thyestes is unwittingly tricked into eating the flesh of his own sons, you have just slept with the woman who entrapped your lover. Even being so kind as to stroke her hair afterward!"

My heart was now racing. Up until a moment ago, I had been trying to console her, making gentle love to her.

". . . So, who killed Akiko?"

"Hm? Oh, your hypothesis was right. My brother wouldn't kill anyone. But when the accident happened, he took the photos—he said *he thought it was a lucky coincidence.* But apparently the photos were failures. He said the model was no good. It's not surprising, with a girl like her."

My vision had narrowed, just like when I found out about your death. But now her body was moving in close to mine again.

"Listen, I'll tell you something else . . . You know how you worried too much about Akiko Yoshimoto? That was your obsession. Your own pathological urge. Okay? Get this: *the reason you fell in love with her was so that you could worry about her.* Something in you needed to suffer through the pain."

At that moment, a tender part of me broke into tattered little pieces.

"But that's all over now. You pity-fucked the person who entrapped the woman you loved. You are no longer yourself. Now fuck me with your intense hatred. Let's see which lasts longer. Fuck me. Hard. Fuck the shit out of me. You hate me, don't you? That's the kind of guy I like. Come on, you hate me, right? I want you to fuck the shit out of me."

As she said this, there was a strange dark glimmer in her eyes. With her lips parted, she smiled, still looking me in the eyes defiantly. As if she was lit from somewhere overhead, I was flooded with the feeling that she seemed to be floating before me. She pressed her lips to mine. And then I fucked her hard. At first, it felt like I was moving involuntarily; I was trembling so badly I though I might collapse. But, inside my head, I was very calm and composed. That was the moment when the plan I've had in mind all along began to take shape within my consciousness. In that instant, I became a monster. It almost felt as though my body were remotely detached from my self. Like I was quietly slipping away. The moment I had felt that vague fear, my body trembled as if denying it, but by the time I had the awareness to say to myself, *Right now I am trembling*, my consciousness had already cooled, like it was already falling away. I felt only a momentary fear toward the version of myself that would be left behind. I could no longer sense any sort of braking mechanism that would help me to maintain balance in my awareness. I must have altered something in me so that I might pit myself against this monstrous brother and sister, so that I might outrival them. Despite the steady calming of my consciousness, a smile remained pasted on my lips. Without any brakes, a person's consciousness was likely capable of transforming into anything. As if circuits had been formed, where they had previously not existed, and were transmitting a strange heat within me. I had sex with her over and over again that night. With intense single-mindedness, and without any hesitation, yet all the while maintaining a strangely cool composure.

The following day, I went to see that lawyer. His sole purpose in life had been vengeance against Akari. He both loved and hated her, and could think of nothing but murdering her. I continued to have sex with Akari regularly while I stayed in contact with the lawyer. In what seemed like a symbolic gesture, he had surveilled me from afar when I first met Akari, but then gradually, almost as if he were tracing a circle, he seemed to have closed the distance as he watched us. Like in Goethe's *Faust*, the way the demon Mephistopheles draws ever closer to

Faust . . . He was crazy in that particular way that stalkers are. Together we worked out our plan. Incidentally, Akari had never lost anyone whom she loved. There were only the two men who had been dumped by her and had then killed themselves.

The lawyer guy had found a woman. She worked in the sex trade, and was drowning in debt. Yuriko Kurihara. Apparently she had graduated from a prestigious high school in Tokyo; goes to show you never really know how life is going to turn out. She might have been able to work out some kind of arrangement with her debts, but she had borrowed the money from someone she had a personal relationship with, and this person was connected to gangsters, and so there was no way for her escape unless she paid it back. There were several reasons why the lawyer had taken pains to select her from among the countless unhappy women here in Japan who are buried in debt. She had no relatives, she was similar in height and body type to Akari Kiharazaka, and somewhat resembled her, too.

This was our plan.

Even if the photos of you, Akiko, were delivered to the police, Yudai Kiharazaka wouldn't be sentenced to die. But if the same thing were to happen again, and if it were clearly a murder, then there was a good chance they'd revisit the first "accident" and it would be ruled a homicide. What's more, together with the longshot photographs of you that he actually took—not the composites—it's likely that the first accident would also be acknowledged as premeditated. Yuriko Kurihara wanted to acquire a new identity. I wanted revenge against Yudai and Akari Kiharazaka. And the lawyer wanted revenge on Akari. And so . . .

We would burn his sister Akari, right before his eyes, so that Yudai Kiharazaka thought it was Yuriko Kurihara.

By doing this to Yudai Kiharazaka, the exact same fate that befell you would befall his sister, Akari. When it happened to you, his photographs didn't capture it. If we planted Yuriko Kurihara with him, even had them living together, and if Yuriko Kurihara were set on fire before him, would he just keep taking photos as before, never realizing she was really his sister? Until she were no more than ashes? Acknowledged as having brutally burned two women to death, the media would have a field day covering the murders, and he would get the death penalty. We would create the evidence that proved he was the one who did it. No one would think that two fires in a row both just happened to be accidents. I knew it. He was in a precarious situation, easy to frame. In short, *we could get him sentenced to death without his having actually killed anyone.*

However, there were obvious objections raised regarding this plan.

The lawyer and I, we weren't planning simply to kill them. Our intention was to inflict cruelty on them. That was why we devised this plan, yet Yuriko Kurihara was quite opposed to it.

For one thing, what would we do if Yudai Kiharazaka, faced with Yuriko (actually Akari) on fire before him, went and tried to save her?

Another factor was, in this day and age of such scientific forensic investigation, would it really be possible to switch the murder victim?

If he were to save Yuriko (actually Akari), then our plan would come to nothing. He would discover that it was his sister who had been burned, and with Akari's testimony, everything would be brought to light. The lawyer, Yuriko, and I would be charged with attempted murder. I was certain that Yudai Kiharazaka would just take photos without trying to save his model, and the lawyer—who was pretty familiar with Kiharazaka's tendencies at this point—was of the same opinion, but Yuriko didn't know Kiharazaka well and kept up her objections. That was how we decided that if Yudai Kiharazaka tried to save his sister, the lawyer would shoot him with a pistol. Then the lawyer would set his sister on fire again. The course of our plan would fall through but, ultimately, the two of them would both be dead anyhow. As it happened, Kiharazaka did just go on taking photos, so there was no need to kill him with the pistol. The ironic thing is, because he took those photos of his sister burning, he was able to extend his life, at least until his execution. Had we killed him with a gun, it would have been quite an inscrutable crime scene. A burnt corpse, the photographer who had apparently filmed it, yet the photographer had been shot dead . . . The investigation might have found us out, or we might have been able to get away. But at least for the lawyer and me, it didn't matter what happened after our plan transpired.

The second factor was the viability of switching the murder victim. But this was comparatively simple. All I had to do was marry Yuriko Kurihara.

She and I were married for appearance's sake. That's how she went from being Yuriko Kurihara to Yuriko Kobayashi. If Yudai Kiharazaka was going to take the photos, then accordingly the building would be severely damaged in the fire. Left at the scene would be Kiharazaka, camera in hand, and a completely burned corpse that had been slowly and carefully doused with kerosene and fire accelerant. The woman's body would be wearing Yuriko Kobayashi's clothing. The clothing would burn completely but maybe the fragment of a button might remain. Naturally, Yudai Kiharazaka would think the burnt body was Yuriko Kobayashi. That's what he would tell the police. But they wouldn't know for sure that it was Yuriko Kobayashi just by someone seeing it firsthand.

In order to officially confirm whether the burnt corpse was Yuriko Kobayashi or not, they would contact Kobayashi's family. That was me, her husband, since she didn't have any parents or siblings or relatives. Bawling my eyes out, I'd stoop over her dead body. This was the ring she was wearing, and this button on her clothing, I'd say tearfully. But the police, seeking conclusive evidence, would probably ask if I had something that might contain a strand of her hair or the like. So that, if possible, they could test it for DNA. Without any protest, I would then hand it over to them. A strand from Akari Kiharazaka's comb. I'd say it was Yuriko's hair . . . Of course the DNA would match.

There was one last thing to make sure of. Verification of her dental records.

I thought it would probably be enough for the distraught husband to identify her body, but we needed to make doubly sure.

Dental records are often used as a means of identifying bodies. Although the theory often used is that if the position of the teeth are the same as in the records then it probably is safe to say they are a match, the fact is that dental records are not always treated as incontrovertible evidence at trial. What's more, dental records in Japan are not compiled in a nationwide database. Each dentist still has their own method of keeping patients' charts. That means the police have to go to the victim's dental clinic to see the records.

So I made a point of telling Akari that she would be even more of a beauty if she fixed up her teeth. Then I sent her to get a simple teeth whitening at a small dental clinic run by an acquaintance of the lawyer, and while she was there, even though she didn't have any cavities, he checked her teeth to make sure. Now they would have Akari's dental records. All we had to do was change the name on the chart to Yuriko Kobayashi. Then those teeth would be registered as belonging to her. The police would go to the dental clinic. They would see the chart there with Yuriko Kobayashi's name on it. Those dental records would of course be identical to those of the burnt corpse. I didn't think it was necessary to go to those lengths and, as it turned out, it wasn't. But the lawyer and I, we were caught up in our own kind of madness. Sometimes madness gives rise to tenaciousness and an obsession with details. I now applied the same fixation as when I had insistently worried about you to the task of strengthening our plan.

This dentist was a troubled man. Around the time when the lawyer had attempted suicide because of Akari, he had taken on a number of clients who had similar difficulties. He had resolved the dentist's financial problems through fairly illicit means. The dentist was greatly indebted to the lawyer and vulnerable to him. But since all he had to do was change the name on a chart, this required relatively little effort when compared with such a debt.

One of the reasons the lawyer had chosen Yuriko Kobayashi was that she bore a certain resemblance to Akari. Which was why he was sure that Yudai Kiharazaka would take a liking to her. *I'm a fan of yours*—that was how Yuriko approached him. *I'm working freelance as a model. For my next job, I want you to take photos of me. Well, the job is just an excuse. Really, I only wanted a reason to talk to you. I saw a picture of you in a magazine article about your photograph* Butterflies . . .

She casually mentioned how attractive the opposite sex seemed to find her. The suggestion made him gradually start to look at her lustfully. Yuriko Kobayashi was definitely beautiful. It was easy to seduce a starving man. Akari was beautiful too, but she was also a terrifying woman. If Yuriko's life hadn't been shackled by her debts, she might have ruined quite a number of men herself.

At the beginning of January, we had her start keeping a diary. A diary that portrayed her as an ordinary housewife. An ordinary housewife who wouldn't give up on her dream of becoming a model. We had her write that she might be being followed. And then the day after she started staying at Yudai Kiharazaka's house, we had her temporarily stop writing in her diary.

We had her do the same thing on Twitter. On Twitter, she hid the fact that she was a housewife, pretending that she was just a woman who worked as a model. As if she were living out her fantasy life in a virtual world. As if just by looking at her diary and Twitter account, however ordinary she may seem, you could tell how likable she was. Then she suddenly stopped tweeting after she started staying at Yudai Kiharazaka's house. And we made a point of sending her all the way to Chiba once, and had her shut off her cell phone there.

All of these things come from the lawyer's madness and my own. We were both morbidly and relentlessly fixated on the details.

At the place where she had worked in the sex trade, of course she had used a false name. Since she hadn't borrowed any money from that place itself, she was able to tell them she was taking a leave of absence. The lawyer and I took over the monthly payments on her debts. She read many of the books that I recommended. We talked about lots of stuff other than the plan. I figured we ought to know at least some things about each other.

About four days after she started staying at Kiharazaka's house, I went to talk to the police. *Once before, she was gone for about a week without any contact. She can be a little emotionally unstable. If she knew that I had gone to the police, she'd be angry with me. That's why I wasn't sure whether or not to file a missing person's report. Yet I can't help but worry . . .*

The police asked me if there was any sign that she was with another man. I acted flustered. It was probably true, but I didn't want to think so, nor could I believe it . . . The police said, rather perfunctorily, that if I wanted to file a missing person's report I needed to say so, and I pretended to be at a loss and went home, only to return two days later with a photo of her when I filed the report. Being that it wasn't a criminal case and was most likely a disappearance involving an extramarital affair, I knew that the police wouldn't take it seriously. It's only after an incident has occurred that police in Japan start doing anything in earnest. Despite how many women are murdered by stalkers they have reported beforehand, the police still haven't changed the way they respond.

Nevertheless, even when they made a serious effort, I doubted they'd be able to make the connection between Yudai Kiharazaka and my "wife." She still had with her the diary that would later become evidence, and her husband—me—wasn't supposed to know that she had starting using Twitter. Even when they investigated her cell phone records, all they could see was that her phone had been turned off somewhere outside of Tokyo. Anyway that would fall under the jurisdiction of the Chiba police, not the Tokyo Metropolitan police department.

Yuriko Kobayashi was playing a dangerous game. But she had no choice other than to go along with our scheme. Here before her was the chance to escape a life in the sex trade, drowning in debt, for a life where she might attain a certain degree of affluence. Akari Kiharazaka didn't have a driver's license or a passport. The only things that could prove her identity were her insurance card and her pension account book, along with the sort of certificate of residence that was archived in the local government office. None of these included a head-shot. As long as Kobayashi had Akari's insurance card and her pension account book, she could request an official copy of her family register from the municipal office where her permanent residence is as if it were her own, and with a copy of her resident card she could then apply for and receive a passport with a photo of herself attached. Why is it that insurance cards in Japan don't have photos? Or why don't they require people to carry a photo ID? Wouldn't it be a good strategy for the auto industry if a driver's license became the typical form of identification? I don't know, but it seems like there are a number of major loopholes like this in the system here in Japan. But then again, even with a photo attached, any number of documents can be forged. And if Yuriko Kobayashi were to die, her debts would be discharged, and she could go on living as Akari Kiharazaka. I was never really worried, despite the fact that I was now her husband, because even though it was a personal loan from a gangster, I wasn't a cosigner, and what's more, it was an illegal contract to start with, so there wouldn't be any obligation to pay it. Because of the kind of person Akari was, she didn't have any friends. And since she lived off of her inheritance, she didn't have a job either. She was a woman on her own in Tokyo, a woman who occasionally lured a man into her solitary life. I often wondered, if she were to disappear, would anyone other than her brother Yudai even notice?

I knew that the PIN number for her ATM card was 0789, and that the one for her credit card was 2289. Yuriko Kobayashi would be able to assume her identity and live her life indefinitely. After the incident, she could go into hiding to avoid the media, while providing her "brother" with that lawyer and leaving Yudai Kiharazaka to take the brunt of it all. Later, when the time was right, she could get a passport and disappear to South America, where she had always yearned to visit.

But there would be major discrepancies between the diary Yuriko Kobayashi left behind and Yudai Kiharazaka's testimony. That's why we decided to have her ask him to kill her.

"Even just sometimes, I want to die. Maybe when I die, I'll think of you. Then take a picture of the place where I die." "I'm kidding—what I said before was a joke. I don't want to die yet." ". . . I don't know why, I just want to give it all up." "I feel like I'm being held prisoner by you . . . I'm kidding, it's a joke—what am I talking about?" ". . . I'm running out of pills. I need more." "You want me to die? But wait. I'll write a suicide note, that way it won't cause any trouble for you." "I hate you. I'm kidding, I love you."

Looking back on it now, it seems like she was protecting herself by being the one to bring up "death" herself. Because in Yudai Kiharazaka's mind, her murder—and his retaking of the photographs he had failed at—was clearly supposed to happen. But, if she were going to write a suicide note, then it was best to wait until then. Looking at it from Kiharaza-ka's perspective, she must have seemed like an emotionally unstable woman. She took a lot of pills in front of him. But they were just vitamins.

We also prepared the notes for her to throw out the window because her legs were tied and she was being held captive. We cut locks of hair. Akari's hair. Naturally, this hair would be identical to the DNA of the dead body.

While Akari Kiharazaka was abusing and heaping invective upon me, at her core, she was falling for me. Of course, the feelings that she had for me were nothing more than her own particular kind of sentimentality. She came to me for sex repeatedly. You probably think that I would have been disgusted to be with a woman like her. But, well, I wasn't. To be honest, I enjoyed it—sleeping with a woman that I knew was going to die soon. I enjoyed it even as I pitied her. It was as if my feelings of pity spiced up the sex. Giving sexual pleasure to someone whom I would soon kill, I had the feeling of having control over this woman, of being able to do whatever I liked. I was no longer the person I had been. I needed to become even more monstrous than this brother and sister. I was forcing myself to become accustomed to this version of me.

Even when you told me that you were leaving me, I still didn't feel like we had parted. Not even when you died, strange as it may sound. That's why I thought I could live with your doll . . . It wasn't until last winter that I finally felt apart from you. That night when I first slept with Akari Kiharazaka. The night when I resolved to become a monster. *Someone who is your boyfriend should not be a monster.* Isn't that right? Last winter, we parted, and I decided to become a monster. I ceased being the person I was. I destroyed myself, so that I could take revenge on them.

. . . I'll tell you about the night when we put Akari Kiharazaka to sleep. I wrapped a towel around her face, blindfolding her. That kind of thing excited her. Then, while we were having sex, I switched places. With the lawyer. The lawyer got undressed and approached Akari, who had no idea.

Had she realized that I had switched with someone else, she probably would have enjoyed it. That's the kind of woman she was. But surely she never would have thought that the guy she was screwing was the guy she had oppressed and treated like an insect.

I smoked a cigarette in the next room, thinking about how strange it was that I didn't feel anything.

When I went back into the room, the lawyer was already wearing his suit and waiting for me. She was knocked out and her hands and feet were tied up. After that, we held her captive for a few days. I couldn't decide whether or not to send the video we had shot to Yudai Kiharazaka. If I sent it to him, despite his suspicions, he might still be aroused by the film, even without knowing that the man her sister was screwing in the film was the lawyer she had made to suffer.

The day of the crime. Strangely, I was not nervous. Based on my long hours of observation, I had a good grasp on Yudai Kiharazaka's behavioral patterns. Since he wasn't actually holding Yuriko Kobayashi captive, while he was out, we went into his studio and made sure that everything was progressing according to plan. We had made sure to have a duplicate key. Our crime took place on the day after Yuriko Kobayashi had mentioned in her diary how lately Yudai Kiharazaka had gotten bored with her, and she had the definite sense that he intended to kill her. We would set fire to his sister just as Kiharazaka was returning home and then leave through a window. It was simple. I had the lawyer film it all. Like I said before, as a precaution for any unexpected situations, he carried a pistol.

I didn't think that what we were doing was all that strange. Within the monster I had become, the part of me that retained a trace of humanity may have dimmed any memory as a means of protecting myself. Then again, I may just be maintaining a certain outward appearance. But, you know, that's a lie. I remember everything clearly. I remember joking with Yuriko Kobayashi, peering at her through the camera lens and shouting at her to hurry up and get Akari ready. I remember, over the course of a few days, whenever Akari would wake up from the slumber we had put her in, knocking her out again until it was time, to the point where she was almost anesthetized, almost like she was dead inside that huge trunk. I remember how I didn't feel the least hesitation at the moment when we set the flames on her. I remember my hand moving as if I were just setting fire to some pieces of cardboard that had been lying around. Striking the match, slowly bringing my arm up from below, and then releasing it from my fingers. Watching the flame as it was about to descend on her, I was thinking to myself: This is what I did it for. I changed who I was so that I could raise my arm this effortlessly and toss the flame just so. I felt like I could do it again, even another time after that. I even vaguely remembered what had happened during the countless times we had experimented. First to burn was the surface of the cloth doused in kerosene. The cloth was flame resistant. But, of course, only to an extent—the material caught fire and when the flames reached Akari and the sofa cushions on which she was lying, which had been doused with even more kerosene, everything ignited fiercely in an instant. We had used ignitable liquid as well as accelerant. The entire sofa was feverishly engulfed in intense flames.

Later when I saw the film, I thought it still seemed a little dangerous. Because when he came into the room, the fire had yet to grow as big as we thought it would. No matter how many times we rehearsed, the perfect timing was quite difficult to achieve. Seeing it from his shaken perspective, with the entire back of the sofa consumed in flames and her arm flung out, it must have looked like her body was already on fire. But in fact the fire had yet to spread to Akari's body under the cloth that we had laid over her. If at that point he had pulled on the arm that was poking out, even though they both would have sustained burns, I bet he could have easily saved his own sister. But, sure enough, he took photographs instead. I felt as though I was watching the same scene as when you had died. Except, of course, this film had transformed it into an act of revenge. The lawyer had the pistol and had been watching closely from outside, but by taking his photos, Kiharazaka narrowly escaped death, even if only for a little while.

After it was all finished, we had Yuriko Kobayashi undergo minor plastic surgery. We fixed the parts of her face that had always bothered her, making them look just right. We didn't try to make her look exactly like Akari Kiharazaka. That would have been impossible, plus I had confirmed with Akari numerous times that she had made her brother destroy all the photos of herself, and she hadn't let him take any photos of her since they had grown up. She said that she hated the way it seemed to capture her true nature. Since from then on she had avoided having any photographs taken; if we were to destroy the few photos that she herself still had, then basically the only quasi-available photographs by which to confirm what she looked like would be her school yearbooks. And those were from quite a while ago.

The problem would be when the police tried to contact

Yudai Kiharazaka's sister to speak to her about her younger brother, that kind of thing. At that point, she shouldn't look like Yukiko Kobayashi, whom Yudai Kiharazaka had photographed and was presumed dead. We cut her hair and dyed it black, and as for the minor plastic surgery, we just had her eyes made bigger and had a mole removed. Then, the only time she met with the police, we had her wear glasses without any makeup. Akari had always been the kind of woman who wore heavy makeup. Naturally, it would have been preferable to have more extensive surgery, but what we did was easily manageable and, when the lawyer and I saw her, we both felt like this was sufficient. The young detective who met with her may have thought that there was a vague resemblance between this "sister" and the photo of Yuriko Kobayashi, and may have thought that was the reason Kobayashi was targeted by this photographer. The police weren't going to haul out an old yearbook to confirm what the "sister" looked like; being neither a victim nor a suspect, this "sister" was nothing more than the sibling of the perpetrator.

After Yudai Kiharazaka was arrested, he said that she set herself on fire. That she had been suicidal and, without waiting for his agreement, had done it herself. However, as a man who had previously had a similar "accident," there was no credibility to what he said. When they showed him the diary Yuriko Kobayashi left behind, he said that she must have even been afraid of him. He ended up testifying that she was emotionally unstable and had accused him of holding her captive. Nobody believed him. The fact that he suffered from manic-depression also worked against him. To top it off, he had hired a lawyer at the request of his "sister." Presumed to be an ally, this lawyer was in fact one of the guys who had framed him for everything. Everything at the trial worked against him.

It was not good that, after setting fire to "Yuriko Kobayashi," he had tried to destroy the evidence. The truth was, after seeing the photographs, he was stunned he had failed yet again. But he still couldn't bring himself to throw away his work, and just like before, he had simply sent the film to the doll creator. Among those photos, there were more composites. This time they were from before the incident. Composite study photographs, almost like practice shots for the kind of photographs he wanted to create if there were a next time, when Yuriko Kobayashi would be on fire. He did that kind of thing, preparatory composites before a shoot, a lot. But his fatal move was not contacting the police or the fire department right away.

His "sister" didn't come to see him; she was admitted into a psychiatric hospital. The only ones left who would know she wasn't Akari when they saw her were her brother and the guys whom she had dumped, but just to be on the safe side, it was better not to let anyone see her. She wrote a letter, the contents imitating what Akari would write. Of course, she couldn't write exactly the same way. A specialist would have seen through it right away. But who's going to avidly remember such details about their own sibling's exact hand-writing in this age of email? If she made the appropriate effort in her mimicry, no one would notice.

This is something I found out later, but apparently he wanted to die. He may have even attempted suicide. When the incident with you occurred, despite the fact that it was an acci-dent, even though he was saved, I bet a part of him felt like he had "murdered" you. He said as much to his sister, that after-ward it was just as if he had killed you himself. And then he did it again. The exact same thing. He didn't have the courage to actually die, so they were going to kill him. That must have been the way he thought about his death sentence.

I think that the real reason for his death wish was probably because of his slump. At the time, he couldn't seem to take any more decent photographs. *Butterflies* was his last one. The pho-tography that drove him mad was his whole life. And then, he had failed at capturing someone's death in a photograph. Even when faced with such brutally compelling "raw material," he managed to take only mediocre photos.

He would never be like the painter he so admired in "Hell Screen."

In the end, he would never ultimately become "authentic."

In other words, this "incident" has revisited upon the brother and sister the same acts that they did to us. I had slept with his sister, not knowing that she had collaborated in the death of my beloved. Blindfolded, the sister had gasped and panted with the guy she herself had oppressed. We did the exact same thing to the dear sister of the brother that he had done to you, Akiko. And then, by this very act, boldly confronted with the drying up of his own talent and awash in the public's hatred, the brother was sentenced to be executed, without having actually killed a single person.

I thought, when this was all over, I would experience some kind of revelation about good and evil, but it's strange . . . I don't feel anything at all.

It's funny, even though I'm sure I've become a monster . . . I still love you, even now.

11

THE HUGE CLOCK hanging on the wall seems to have stopped moving.

"I think I want to quit working on this project."

The moment I say it, I feel a small pang of regret, along with a calm sense of release. My editor gazes across at me, looking slightly dazed.

"Why . . . ?"

". . . It's too much for me. I'm sorry."

"I want you to explain to me, specifically. What happened?"

We are at my editor's apartment. I stare at the glass of

whiskey on the table. My editor is staring at the same thing. He lights a cigarette. I remain silent.

". . . You mean, you're in over your head?"

I look at the unmoving clock on the wall. It seems disproportionately large for the room. He opens his mouth to speak.

"Have you read Truman Capote's *In Cold Blood*?"

". . . I have."

"After he completed his nonfiction novel, he couldn't write another decent piece of work. His spirit was broken. Then again, at least he did finish that book."

Yudai Kiharazaka's sister had said something very similar to me. My heart starts to race. My editor raises his voice slightly.

"Sure, the way that I do things may be relentless. Some have even called me pathological because I always push a writer beyond the limits of his abilities. And as a result, some writers' spirits have broken. But I just want to make a good book. That's all. It may sound callous, but I'm not thinking about the writer. The only thing I care about it is the work."

"I understand that."

"Really?"

The editor looks me straight in the eyes.

"Capote managed to write his all. He put his heart and soul into it. And you—you're going to give up at this point?"

He still isn't finished with what he has to say.

"Well, this is frustrating. I'm disappointed to hear your position. It sounds like you're putting your personal life above your own work. Get out of here."

He takes another drag from his cigarette.

"Don't bother sending me your expenses. This will be a major loss for us. And I don't want to deal with you anymore."

"I might have walked away, pretending that I didn't know anything . . ."

Despite what I say, the editor is still puffing on his cigarette. I take a deep breath in order to calm my growing nervousness.

"Akari Kiharazaka showed me the photograph."

My throat feels dry as I speak.

"The photo of her from long ago, the only one that Yudai Kiharazaka had kept . . . It was of a girl I didn't recognize. It was completely different from the photo of her and her brother that Akari Kiharazaka had shown me previously. That is to say . . . the first photo was a composite. To make it seem like she was Yudai Kiharazaka's sister. To fool me."

The editor is looking me in the face.

"That's not all. The photos that you first showed me of Akari Kiharazaka were of her passing herself off as the 'sister.' You made sure to make them seem like they had been supplied by the Kiharazakas. Actual photographs that show what Akari Kiharazaka really looks like probably don't exist anymore.

Except for elementary or junior high school yearbooks and that one photo of her when she was a girl that she still has, the one that her brother saved. And so I had no reason not to believe, as I was told, that she was Akari Kiharazaka . . . Also there were no photos of Yuriko Kobayashi released to the public. The media withheld them due to the strongly expressed wishes of the 'bereaved family.' And in the archives I received from you, the one person there weren't any photos of was Yuriko Kobayashi. And even the photos of her after she had become Akari—you only showed me those briefly, you didn't hand them over."

The temperature in the room grew chilly.

"She told me. That she was only pretending to be the 'sister.' That she had been blackmailed by a man. Save me, she said . . . It was creepy, it didn't make any sense. I went to see the doll maker, too. He had the photographs of Akiko Yoshimoto and Yuriko Kobayashi on fire. And there was a doll in his collection that looked familiar. A doll of the first victim, Akiko Yoshimoto. He drew me a portrait of the person who commissioned its production—the face of the man who was Akiko Yoshimoto's former boyfriend. It was you."

The editor lowers his gaze and brings the glass of whiskey to his lips.

"I realized that you were involved in this incident. It occurred to me that perhaps it might be some kind of revenge. When

I looked at the photos again, the ones of Yuriko Kobayashi when she was on fire, her eyes were quite different and the impression was completely different too, yet I thought she bore a vague resemblance to the 'sister.' I was confused and, at the same time, I had a terrible foreboding. Having been shown the 'composites' once, something told me that these photographs of Yuriko Kobayashi burning might also be composites. But I didn't know why these photographs existed. If I was right, that would mean that Yuriko Kobayashi was alive. The truth was, a woman who looked a lot like her was living as Kiharazaka's sister. That meant that, all along, I had been seeing Yuriko Kobayashi posing as the sister. Yuriko Kobayashi, who was supposed to be dead, was pretending to be Kiharazaka's sister. So the person who was actually burned . . . There was only one answer. Identifying the body is done by the family. I had thought it was a mere coincidence that you and Yuriko Kobayashi had the same family name."

I draw in my breath again.

"I was told that Yuriko Kobayashi, posing as the sister, contacted the doll maker by phone, saying that she wanted to reclaim all of the photos Kiharazaka had taken, as well as the Akiko Yoshimoto doll. As far as she was concerned, she wanted to hush up everything. That doll connected you to this incident. And that made it a piece of evidence that would connect to her. But the doll maker, he interpreted her call to mean something different. That Akari Kiharazaka had used her brother in order to have those women killed. The doll maker didn't know that Akari Kiharazaka was already dead. So he thought that she had made her brother kill them, out of jealousy or something. He figured that there was something mysterious behind all this, but he had his own way of thinking about it. Maybe that Akari was a lesbian, and was trying to get a hold of the doll that had grown more beautiful after the death of the real Akiko Yoshimoto. That's his kind of wacky reasoning."

Still drinking his whiskey, he stares at me.

"But I don't get it. Why did you hire me for this job? Why go to the trouble, of dredging up a crime that you pulled off?"

He doesn't reply. I draw in my breath, holding back the tremor in my voice.

"After I left the doll maker's home, I pressed her for an explanation, and she confessed that she was Yuriko Kobayashi. I didn't know if she was telling the truth or not, but she said that she was being blackmailed. That's why she asked me to run away with her. Take me with you and let's run away together, she said . . . She told me even more. That there was someone she wanted me to kill beforehand. She hinted at it over and over, until finally she put it bluntly."

". . . Okay."

"It's been a while already since you finished that whiskey. She gave it to me. It should take effect soon enough."

He stares at me, the glass still in his hand. Moments pass but he remains calm. Or rather, he appears to be objectively wondering about the fact that he isn't upset. I draw in a short breath to say something, when suddenly he begins to speak.

"Right. She did that. Just out of curiosity, is it sleeping pills that I drank? Or something that it's too late to undo?"

"Something that it's too late to undo."

My eyes meet his. Only for a few seconds, but it feels like much longer.

"So that's how it is."

"But why? Why did she do this to you?"

He gives a terse laugh at what I say.

"You're willing to kill someone without knowing the reason why?"

He leans against the sofa and lights another cigarette. As if he is taking stock of his own body, he raises his arm slightly, casting his gaze over the palm of his right hand.

"Because I was trying to make a book. About what happened."

He brings his gaze back to me.

"I wasn't going to publish anything. I guess I wanted to stop myself, stop this dangerous act of dredging it back up. Even if I die now, it's easy enough to make it seem like it was from grief over my dead 'wife,' isn't it? By the way, how long do I have? Before I die."

I stare at the whiskey in the glass before me. The surface of the amber-colored liquid brightly reflects the light in the room. Slowly, I bring the glass to my lips.

"There's nothing in it. I switched the bottle with another I brought along with me . . . I couldn't do it."

But the editor, he doesn't show any sign of relief. My eyes meet his. A few seconds go by, and I feel like a few minutes more have passed. But then finally, as if weary, he begins to speak softly.

"Your doubts are reasonable. You must have thought it was a strange assignment, to go through the interview process, if possible to write it as you go along, then send it in to me. I was surprised when I read your opening sentence. 'It's safe to say you killed them . . . Isn't that right?' Those words seemed to symbolize this whole 'incident.' But the part about yourself is a bit overwritten. I corrected it here and there. Readers want to know about the writer's personal life. Nevertheless, you don't even mention a single thing about your girlfriend, Yukie. You can't hide yourself and still write. That's why I changed that part too. As well as the fact that you don't delve at all inside of Kiharazaka's mind. That's why I went ahead and started up a correspondence with him. Concealing my true identity, of course. Really, I wanted audio recordings of the interview subjects, but you couldn't even manage to get those. So I had no choice but to rely on your subjectivity. By the time Yudai Kiharazaka wrote to me, asking to *swap stories of our insanity*, it was already over—I had accomplished what I'd planned to do to him."

"But what if I had . . ."

"Gone to the police? You mean when you eventually suspected? Good point. But you're so conscientious, I knew that before going to them, you'd be sure to come to me, just as you have. And when that happened, I could kill you. Just make you write the manuscript . . . You drank the whiskey too, didn't you? There's cyanide on your glass."

I look at the editor, at a loss.

"A lot of corrections had to be made to the manuscript you delivered, but for the most part, it's all there. I liked your writing style. I'm an editor, so I can't make something from nothing. But this is all I need—I can go back later and mimic your style. There wasn't anything in your manuscript about Yuriko Kobayashi trying to kill someone—I think I'll add in some hints about that. The editorial process may take a while."

My heart starts to race and I can no longer see straight. Trembling, I bring my right hand to my mouth and try to stick my fingers down my throat to make myself vomit. I wonder if I still have time. I . . . Suddenly he puts a bottle on the table.

"Don't worry. There wasn't anything on the glass."

He smiles.

"Well . . . I thought about it. Look, I've got some potassium cyanide. But I changed my mind. Just like you did. I wonder why."

The temperature in the room is getting even chillier. It takes a little while for me to realize that I have been staring, dumbfounded, at the editor all this time. I have broken out into a sweat all over my body, to an embarrassing extent. He is staring at me now.

"Is it because you saw the graves?"

". . . The graves?"

"Yeah. The graves of Yudai and Akari Kiharazaka's mother and father."

He is still leaning far back on the sofa.

"If you had looked them up, you would have seen what their parents were like when the kids were little. A quite simple man, violently alcoholic, and a woman who disappears, leaving behind her children. The soil into which they were born definitely nurtured them into what they became. I thought I needed to seek revenge upon those parents as well, and when it was all over, I aimlessly searched for their whereabouts. But I ended up at two graves. They were old and small, and no one had left any flowers. They were overgrown with weeds . . . While I was there, a strange feeling came over me. After I had taken revenge on the ones who were in these graves, I would need to seek revenge on their parents as well—that's how I felt."

He smiles.

"The fact was, I didn't feel an ounce of regret about what I did to the brother and sister. But I just sat there for a while. I could feel the air around me as it moved softly over my cheeks and my hands . . . I was there for hours."

As he speaks, he brings the glass of whiskey to his lips again.

"My sorrow, hatred, and joy—all of it was ending. Eventually my life would go on. Like the breeze that moved tranquilly amongst the small stone graves . . . Just what does it all mean? This world we live in."

I light a cigarette.

"By the way, what do you intend to do, now that you've quit this project?"

"I'm going to marry Yukie. And then, I've got work as a celebrity ghostwriter."

My voice quavers slightly.

"When I figured out what was going on with you and them, I was reminded of that photograph, *Butterflies*. What's inside each person, the true desire that people aren't even aware of . . . Yudai Kiharazaka had no desires of his own. His envy of others, that imitation was all there was for him. That was even what led him to just want to die. It's terrible, but that was when I figured it all out. It's not my true desire to lead a ruinous life. Desire for something wild and violent is not what creates beautiful art. I want stability—though occasionally I yearn for ruin—and since it doesn't matter to me what kind of work I do, everyone is just a little envious. I realized that I would never be a novelist. That's why I can't write this book about you and them. The 'sister' told me so from the start. She said, You aren't capable of writing a book about us. She said, You cannot simply come into *our realm*. She was right."

"Don't worry. I'll take over. Together you and I will make this into a 'novel.' The only thing I ask of you is to write this scene of us here, if you can."

I stare at my cigarette, which had burned down to a nub.

"I'm quitting smoking from now on. To mark this day, this will be my last cigarette."

I take a drag, and exhale slowly. The white smoke gently drifts away. As if something inside me is quietly emerging. I put out the cigarette in the ashtray. A thin line of smoke rises faintly from the extinguished stub, disappearing before long. There is a smile on the editor's lips.

"That's great. You should take care of yourself. Despite the inherent tedium of the world, it's beautiful to see those people who still live fully. But, every so often, I want you to remember the utter folly of what we did with our lives. And the fact that it was the way we truly wanted to live."

He stands up slowly, still holding his whiskey. He lights yet another cigarette.

"Akari told me. She said that the reason I fell in love with Akiko Yoshimoto was so that I could suffer through the pain of worrying about her. She was a woman who said terrible things. Still . . . whatever the reason, that was all I felt when I fell in love with her, and I wanted to believe it was the real thing. That was the only time . . . when I felt like the world was truly beautiful."

". . . Yes."

"I wonder. If Akiko saw me now . . . what would she do with me?"

I remain seated on the sofa, watching him. He seems far away from where I am.

"It's not simply a duality between either acceptance or rejection, nor between acknowledgment or denial. She . . . I think she might just take you in her arms, tearfully . . . As foolish as you are. But I don't know."

He smiles at what I say.

"Would it really work out that easily . . . ? And what I also wonder . . . well, my actions were unilateral."

He takes a sip of whiskey.

"She liked the books I edited. A long time ago, she said something to me in jest. She said, If I'm ever murdered, like in a mystery novel, I want you to make that into a book. Hunt down my killer, and take revenge for me. She was a very energetic person. I decided to create the 'novel,' and I thought I'd send it first to

Yudai Kiharazaka. It would be a strange mix of archived materials and fiction chapters. This would be after his death sentence had been definitively determined. He would read the novel in prison, and knowing the truth about what had been done to him would likely drive him insane. And thus, my revenge would be complete . . . It's a rather editorial revenge, isn't it? Because he's already crazy, right? He'd make a big commotion, saying it was a conspiracy between the state and the judge, and even though he knew the truth, nobody would pay him any attention. He'd be executed. After his execution, they'll say, maybe there was something strange about that 'novel' . . ."

He is looking off somewhere. I can't tell where.

"And I will dedicate the book to her. She was blind. That's why everything is written out, even the video archives. Later it would all need to be put into Braille. That's why I'd write their names on the first page of the story. A dedication, like in foreign novels . . . But because the Japanese are easily embarrassed, I'd use the alphabet. Since it's a 'novel,' I used aliases in the main part of the book, but these would be their real initials. The first one would be for the photographer on death row, and then for my beloved."

He is still looking off somewhere.

"It would be just like the book itself: on the one hand, a manifestation of pure hatred, and on the other, a manifestation of true love . . . Dedicated to M.M, and to J.I."